"If You Can't Be Nice And At Least *Pretend* To Smile, You'll Just Have To Go Away."

"Oh, for God's sake." Simon had had enough of this. He wasn't going to be chastised by anybody, least of all the short, curvy woman giving him a disgusted look.

He stalked across the small kitchen, plucked the baby from Tula's grasp and held Nathan up to eye level. The baby's pout disappeared as if it had never been and the two of them simply stared at each other.

In that instant Simon was lost.

He knew even as he stood there, beneath Tula Barrons's less than approving stare, that this was his son and he would do whatever he had to in order to keep him.

If this woman stood in his way, he'd roll right over her without a moment's pause. Something in his gaze must have given away his thoughts, because the small blonde lifted her chin, met his eyes in a bold stare and told him silently that she wouldn't give an inch.

Fine.

She'd learn soon enough that when Simon Bradley entered a contest—he never lost.

Dear Reader,

All writers are different. But for me, when I've finished writing a book, I'm satisfied with the way my characters' story has played out and I'm ready to move on.

Usually. But Tula Barrons was different. Tula first showed up in my story "The Wrong Brother" in the holiday 2-in-1, *Under the Millionaire's Mistletoe.* Tula was my heroine Annie's best friend. And I loved her so much, I couldn't let her go until she had a story of her own.

So in *Have Baby, Need Billionaire,* Tallulah "Tula" Barrons gets her hero. Tula didn't have a great childhood, but she does have the best attitude ever. She's made her own life and she's happy with it. Until she inherits a baby and falls in love with that little boy's father.

Simon Bradley doesn't know what hit him. Finding a son he didn't know about is a surprise, but the baby's guardian is the one who knocks him for a loop.

Simon is a rules guy. Tula has never met a rule she didn't break. Simon likes order and Tula thrives on chaos. Bringing these two very opposite people together was a lot of fun for me. And this time, when the book was finished, I was happy with Tula's story. I hope you are, too!

Follow me on Facebook, visit my website at www.maureenchild.com or write to me at P.O. Box 1883, Westminster, CA 92684-1883.

Happy reading!

Maureen

MAUREEN CHILD

HAVE BABY, NEED BILLIONAIRE

Published by Silhouette Books
America's Publisher of Contemporary Romance

Recycling programs for this product may not exist in your area.

ISBN-13: 978-0-373-73072-8

HAVE BABY, NEED BILLIONAIRE

This edition published by arrangement with Harlequin Books S.A.

For questions and comments about the quality of this book please contact us at Customer_eCare@Harlequin.ca.

Visit Silhouette Books at www.eHarlequin.com

Printed in U.S.A.

Books by Maureen Child

Silhouette Desire

†*Scorned by the Boss* #1816
†*Seduced by the Rich Man* #1820
†*Captured by the Billionaire* #1826
††*Bargaining for King's Baby* #1857
††*Marrying for King's Millions* #1862
††*Falling for King's Fortune* #1868
High-Society Secret Pregnancy #1879
Baby Bonanza #1893
An Officer and a Millionaire #1915
Seduced Into a Paper Marriage #1946
††*Conquering King's Heart* #1965
††*Claiming King's Baby* #1971
††*Wedding at King's Convenience* #1978
††*The Last Lone Wolf* #2011
Claiming Her Billion-Dollar Birthright #2024
††*Cinderella & the CEO* #2043
Under the Millionaire's Mistletoe #2056
"The Wrong Brother"
Have Baby, Need Billionaire #2059

†Reasons for Revenge
††Kings of California

MAUREEN CHILD

is a California native who loves to travel. Every chance they get, she and her husband are taking off on another research trip. The author of more than sixty books, Maureen loves a happy ending and still swears that she has the best job in the world. She lives in Southern California with her husband, two children and a golden retriever with delusions of grandeur. Visit Maureen's website at www.maureenchild.com.

For Carter
He's never met the Lonely Bunny
But he loves the Little Critters

One

Simon Bradley didn't like surprises.

In his experience, any time a man let himself be taken unawares, disaster happened.

Order. Rules. He was a man of discipline. Which is why it only took one look at the woman standing in his office to know that *she* wasn't his kind of female.

Pretty though, he told himself, his gaze sweeping her up and down in a brisk, detailed look. She stood about five foot four and looked even shorter because she was so delicately made. She was tiny, really, with short blond hair that clung to her head in chunky layers that framed her face. Big silver hoops dangled from her ears and her wide blue eyes were fixed on him thoughtfully. Her mouth was curved in what appeared to be a permanent half smile and a single dimple winked at him from her right cheek. She wore black jeans, black boots and a bright red sweater that molded itself to her slight but curvy body.

He ignored the flash of purely male interest as he met her gaze and stood up behind his desk. “Ms. Barrons, is it? My assistant tells me you insisted on seeing me about something ‘urgent’?”

“Yes, hi. And please, call me Tula,” she said, her words tumbling from her delectable-looking mouth in a rush. She walked toward him, right hand extended.

His fingers folded over hers and he felt a sudden, intense surge of heat. Before he could really question it, she shook his hand briskly, then stepped back. Looking past him at the wide window behind him, she said, “Wow, that’s quite a view. You can see all of San Francisco from here.”

He didn’t turn around to share the view. He watched her instead. His fingers were still buzzing and he rubbed them together to dissipate the sensation. No, she wasn’t his type at all, but damned if he wasn’t enjoying looking at her. “Not all, but a good part of it.”

“Why don’t you have your desk facing the window?”

“If I did that, I’d have my back to the door, wouldn’t I?”

“Right.” She nodded then shrugged. “Still, I think it’d be worth it.”

Pretty, but disorganized, he thought. He glanced at his wristwatch. “Ms. Barrons—”

“Tula.”

“Ms. Barrons,” he said deliberately, “if you’ve come to talk about the view, I don’t really have time for this. I’ve got a board meeting in fifteen minutes and—”

“Right. You’re a busy man. I get that. And no, I didn’t

come to talk about the view, I got a little distracted, that's all."

Distractions, he thought wryly, *are probably how this woman lives her life.* She was already letting her gaze slide around his office rather than getting to the point of her visit. He watched her as she took in the streamlined office furniture, the framed awards from the city and the professionally done photos of the other Bradley department stores across the country.

Pride rose up inside him as he, too, took a moment to admire those photos. Simon had worked hard for the last ten years to rebuild a family dynasty that his father had brought to the brink of ruin. In one short decade, Simon had not only regained ground lost, thanks to his father's sloppy business sense, he'd taken the Bradley family chain of upscale shopping centers further than anyone else ever had.

And he hadn't accomplished all of that by being distracted. Not even by a pretty woman.

"If you don't mind," he said, coming around his desk to escort her personally to the door, "I am rather busy today...."

She flashed him a full smile and Simon felt his heart take an odd, hard lurch in his chest. Her eyes lit up and that dimple in her cheek deepened and she was suddenly the most beautiful thing he'd ever seen. Shaken, Simon brushed that thought aside and told himself to get a grip.

"Sorry, sorry," Tula said, waving both hands in the air as if to erase her own tendency to get sidetracked. "I really am here to talk to you about something very important."

"All right then, what is it that's so urgent you vowed to

spend a week in my waiting area if you weren't allowed to speak to me immediately?"

She opened her mouth, shut it again, then suggested, "Maybe you should sit down."

"Ms. Barrons…"

"Fine," she said with a shake of her head. "Your call. But don't say I didn't warn you."

Pointedly, he glanced at his watch.

"I get it," she told him. "Busy man. You want it and you want it now. Okay then, here it is. Congratulations, Simon Bradley. You're a father."

He stiffened and any sense of courtesy went out the window along with his sense of bemused tolerance. "Your five minutes are up, Ms. Barrons." He took her elbow in a firm grip and steered her toward the door.

Her much shorter legs were moving fast, trying to either keep up or slow him down, he wasn't sure which. Either way, it didn't make a difference to him. Beautiful or not, whatever game she was playing, it wasn't going to work. Simon was no one's father and he damn well knew it.

"Hey!" She finally dug the heels of her boots into the lush carpet and slowed his progress a bit. "Wait a second! Geez, overreact much?"

"I'm not a father," he ground out tightly. "And trust me when I say that if I had ever slept with you, I would remember."

"I didn't say I was the baby's mother."

He didn't listen. Just kept moving toward the door at a relentless pace.

"I would have worked up to that little declaration slower, you know," she was babbling. "You're the one who wanted it direct and fast."

"I see. This was for my benefit."

"No, it's for your son's benefit, you boob."

He staggered a little in spite of knowing that she had to be lying. A son? Impossible.

She took advantage of the momentary pause in his forced march toward the door to break free of his grip and step back just out of reach. He was unsettled enough to let her go. He didn't know what she was trying to pull, but at the moment, her eyes looked soft but determined as she met his gaze.

"I realize this is coming as a complete shock to you. Heck, it would be for anybody."

Simon shook his head and narrowed his eyes on her. Enough of this. He didn't have a son and he wasn't going to fall for whatever moneygrubbing scheme she'd come up with in her delusional fantasies. Best to lay that on the line right from the start.

"I've never even seen you before, Ms. Barrons, so obviously, we don't have a child together. Next time you want to convince someone to pay for a child that doesn't exist, you might want to try it on someone you've actually slept with."

She blinked up at him in confusion, then a moment later she laughed. "No, no. I told you, I'm not the baby's mother. I'm the baby's aunt. But you're definitely his father. Nathan has your eyes and even that stubborn chin of yours. Which does not bode well, I suppose. But stubbornness can often be a good quality, don't you think?"

Nathan.

The imaginary baby had a name.

But that didn't make any of this situation real.

"This is insane," he told her. "You're obviously

after something, so why not just spill it and get it over with."

She was muttering to herself as she walked back to his desk and Simon was forced to follow her. "I had a speech all prepared, you know. You rushed me and everything's confused now."

"I think you're the only thing confused here," Simon told her, moving to pick up his phone and call security. They could escort her out and he'd be done with this and back to work.

"I'm not confused," she said. She read his expression and added, "I'm not crazy, either. Look, give me five minutes, okay?"

He hung up. Wasn't sure why. Maybe it was the gleam in her blue eyes. Maybe it was that tantalizing dimple that continued to show itself and disappear again. But if there was the slightest chance that what she was saying was true, then he owed it to himself to find out.

"All right," he said, checking his watch. "Five minutes."

"Okay." She took a deep breath and said, "Here we go. Do you remember dating a woman named Sherry Taylor about a year and a half ago?"

A thin thread of apprehension slithered through Simon as he searched his memory. "Yes," he said warily.

"Well...I'm Sherry's cousin, Tula Barrons. Actually, Tallulah, named after my grandmother, but that's such a hideous name that I go by Tula...."

He was hardly listening to her now. Instead his mind was focused on those nebulous memories of a woman in his past. Was it possible?

She took another steadying breath and said, "I know

this is hard to take in, but while you two were together, Sherry got pregnant. She gave birth to your son six months ago, in Long Beach."

"She *what?*"

"I know, I know. She should have told you," the woman said, lifting both hands as if to say it wasn't her fault. "I actually tried to convince her to tell you, but she said she didn't want to intrude on your life or anything, so..."

Intrude on his life.

That was an understatement. God, he could barely remember what the woman looked like. Simon rubbed at the spot between his eyes as if somehow that might clear up the foggy memories. But all he came up with was a vague image of a woman who had been in and out of his life in about two weeks' time.

And while he'd gone on his way without a backward glance, she'd been *pregnant?* With *his* child? And didn't even bother to *tell* him?

"What? Why? How?"

"All very good questions," she said, smiling at him again, this time in a sympathetic fashion. "I'm really sorry this is such a shock, but—"

Simon wasn't interested in her sympathy. He wanted answers. If he really did have a son, then he needed to know everything.

"Why now?" he demanded. "Why did your cousin wait until now to tell me, and why isn't she here herself?"

Her eyes filmed over and he had the horrifying thought that she was going to cry. Damn it. He hated when women cried. Made a man feel completely helpless. Not something he enjoyed at all. But a moment later, the woman had gotten control of her emotions and managed to stem the tide of those tears. Her eyes still glittered with them, but she refused to let them fall and Simon found, unexpectedly, that he admired her for it.

"Sherry died a couple of weeks ago," she said softly.

Another quick jolt of surprise in a morning that felt full of them. "I'm sorry," he said, knowing it sounded lame and clichéd, but what else was there to say?

"Thanks," she said. "It was a car accident. She died instantly."

"Look, Ms. Barrons…"

She sighed. "If I *beg,* will you please call me Tula?"

"Fine. Tula," he amended, thinking it really was the least he could do, considering. For the first time in a very long time, Simon had been caught completely off guard.

He wasn't sure how to react. His instinct, of course, was to find this baby and if it was his son, to claim him. But all he had was this stranger's word, along with memories that were too obscure to trust. Why in the hell would a woman get pregnant and not tell the baby's father? Why wouldn't she have come to him if that child really was his?

He scrubbed one hand across his jaw. "Look, I'm sorry to say, I don't really remember much about your cousin. We weren't together long. I don't see why you're so sure this baby is mine."

"Because Sherry named you on the baby's birth certificate."

"She gave the baby my name and didn't bother to tell me?" He didn't even know what to say to that.

"I know," she said, her tone soothing.

He didn't want to be soothed. Or understood. "She could have put anyone's name down," he pointed out.

"Sherry didn't lie."

Simon laughed at the ridiculousness of that statement. "Is that right?"

Tula winced. "All right, fine. She lied to you, but she wouldn't have lied to her son. She wouldn't have lied about Nathan's name."

"Why should I believe that the boy is mine?"

"You did have sex with her?"

Scowling, Simon admitted, "Well, yes, I did, but—"

"And you do know how babies are made, right?"

"That's very amusing."

"I'm not trying to be funny," she told him. "Just honest. Look, you can do a paternity test, but I can tell you that Sherry would never have named you as Nathan's father in her will if she wasn't sure."

"Her will?" The silent clang of a warning bell went off in his mind.

"Didn't I already tell you that part?"

"No."

She shook her head and dropped into one of the chairs angled in front of his desk. "Sorry. It's been a busy couple of weeks for me, what with Sherry's accident and arranging the funeral and closing up her house and moving the baby up here to my house in Crystal Bay."

Sensing that this was going to go on far longer than the original five minutes he'd allowed her, Simon walked around the edge of his desk and took a seat. At the very least, he was now in the position of power. He watched the pretty blonde and asked, "What about the will?"

Tula reached into the oversize black leather bag she had slung over her shoulder. She pulled out a large manila envelope and dropped it onto his desk. "That's a copy of Sherry's will. If you look, you'll see that I've been named temporary guardian of Nathan. Until I'm sure that you're ready to be the baby's father."

Her voice, her words, were no more than a buzz of sound in his head. He read through the will quickly, scanning until he found the provisions for the child Sherry had named as his. *Custody of minor, Nathan Taylor, goes to the child's father, Simon Bradley.*

He sat back in his chair and kept rereading those words until he was fairly certain they'd been burned into his brain. Was this true? Was he a father?

Lifting his gaze to hers, Simon found Tula Barrons studying him through those wide, brilliant blue eyes. She was waiting for him to say something.

Damned if he knew what it should be.

He'd been careful, always, in his relationships with women. He'd had no desire to be a father. And yet he had a vague memory of being with Sherry Taylor. The woman herself was hardly more than a smudge in his memories—but he did remember the night the condom had broken. A man didn't forget things like that. But she'd never said anything about a baby, so he'd forgotten about the incident.

It was possible.

He might really have a son.

Tula watched as Simon Bradley came to terms with a whole new reality.

She gave him points. Sure, he'd been a little edgy, temperamental...all right, *rude,* at first. But she supposed that was to be expected. After all, it wasn't every day you found out you were a father, for heaven's sake.

Her gaze moved over him while he was reading the

will and Tula had to admit that he wasn't at all what she'd been expecting. She and her cousin Sherry hadn't been close, by any means, but Tula would have bet that she would at least know Sherry's taste in men.

And tall, dark, gorgeous and crabby wasn't it. Normally, Sherry had gone for the quiet, sweet, geeky type. Simon was about as far from that description as a man could get. He practically radiated power, strength. Ever since she had walked into the room, Tula had felt a sizzle of attraction for him that she was still battling. She so didn't need yet one more complication at the moment.

"What exactly is it you want from me?"

His voice shattered her thoughts and she met his gaze. "I should think that would be obvious."

He dropped the sheaf of papers to his desktop. "Well, you would be wrong."

"Okay, how about this? Why don't you come out to my place in Crystal Bay? Meet your son. Then we can talk and figure out our next move together."

He scrubbed one hand across the back of his neck. She'd dumped a lot of information on him all at once, Tula told herself. Of course he was going to need a little time to acclimate.

"Fine," he said at last. "What's your address?"

She told him, then watched as he stood up behind his desk in a clear signal of dismissal. Well, that was all right with her. She had things to do anyway and what more was there to say at the moment? Tula stood up, too, and held her right hand out toward him.

A moment's pause, then his hand engulfed hers. Again, just as it had happened earlier, the instant their palms met a bolt of heat shot up her arm and ricocheted around her chest like a manic Ping-Pong ball. He must have felt the same thing because he dropped her hand and shoved his own into his pocket.

She took a breath, blew it out and forced a smile that felt wobbly. "I'll see you tonight then."

As she left, Tula felt his gaze on her and the heat engendered by his stare stayed with her on the long ride home.

Two

"How'd it go?"

Tula smiled at the sound of her best friend's voice. Anna Cameron Hale was the one human being on the face of the planet that Tula could count on being on her side. So, naturally, the moment she'd returned from San Francisco and facing down Simon Bradley, she dialed Anna's number.

"About as you'd expect."

"Ouch," Anna said. "So he had no idea about the baby?"

"Nope." Tula turned to look at Nathan, sitting in his bouncy seat. The babysitter, Mrs. Klein, had said that the baby was "good as gold" the whole time she was gone. Now, as he bounced and pushed off with his toes, the springs squeaked into motion, jolting him up and down in the small kitchen.

Tula's heart gave a little Nathan-caused twinge that she was starting to get used to. How was it possible to love someone so much in the span of a couple of short weeks?

"In his defense, it must have been a shock for him to be faced with this out of the blue," Anna said.

"True. I mean I knew about Nathan and it was still a stunner when Sherry died and suddenly I'm responsible for him." Although, she thought, it hadn't taken more than five minutes for her to adjust. "But when I told Simon, he looked like he'd been hit with a two-by-four."

"God, honey, I'm sorry it didn't go well. So what do you do now?"

"He's coming here tonight to meet Nathan and then we're going to talk." Tula thought briefly about the little buzz of sensation she'd received when he shook her hand and then pushed that thought right out of her mind. There was already plenty going on at the moment. She *so* didn't need anything else to think about.

But her mind couldn't quite keep from remembering him as he stood over her, all fierce and furious.

"He's going to your house?" Anna asked.

Tula shook her head and paid attention. "Yeah, why?"

"Nothing. But maybe I could come over and help you get ready."

She knew exactly what Anna was thinking and Tula couldn't help laughing. "You are not coming over to clean my house. He's not visiting royalty or something."

Anna laughed, too. "Fine. Just warn him when he walks in to watch where he steps."

Tula stepped away from the kitchen counter and shot

a look into her tiny living room. Toys littered the floor, her laptop was sitting open on the coffee table and her latest manuscript was beside it. She was doing revisions for her editor and when she was working, other things—like picking up clutter—tended to go by the wayside.

Shrugging, she silently admitted that though her house was clean, it did tend to get a little messy. Especially now that she had Nathan living with her. She hadn't had any idea just how much *stuff* came along with a baby.

"Why did I call you again?" Tula asked.

"Because I'm your best friend and you know you need me."

"Right, that was it." Tula smiled and reached out one hand to smooth the wispy hairs on the top of Nathan's head as he scooted past, babbling happily. "It was weird, Anna. Simon was crabby and rude and dismissive and yet…"

"Yet *what?*" Anna prompted.

There was a buzz of interest, Tula thought but didn't say. She hadn't expected it, hadn't wanted it, but hadn't been able to ignore it, either. The suit-and-tie kind of guy was *so* not what she was interested in. And for heaven's sake, the last thing she needed was to be attracted to Nathan's father. This situation was hard enough. Yet she couldn't deny the flash of heat that had flooded her system the moment her hand had met his.

Didn't mean she had to do anything about it though, she assured herself firmly.

"Hello?" Anna said. "Finish what you were saying! What comes after the 'yet'?"

"Nothing," Tula said with sudden determination. One thing she didn't need was to indulge in an attraction for a man she had nothing in common with but a baby they were both responsible for. "Absolutely nothing."

"And you expect me to just accept that?"

"As my friend, I'm asking you to, yeah."

Anna sighed dramatically. "Fine. I will. For *now*."

"Thanks." She'd accept the reprieve, even though she knew that Anna wouldn't let it go forever.

"So what're you going to do tonight?"

"Simon comes here and we talk about Nathan. Set something up so that he can get to know the baby and I can watch them together. I can handle Simon," she said a moment later and wasn't sure whether she was trying to convince Anna or herself. "I grew up around men like him, remember?"

"Tula, not every man who wears a suit is like your dad."

"Not all," she allowed, "but most."

She was in the position to know. Her entire family had practically been born wearing business suits. They lived stuffy, insular lives built around making and keeping money. Tula was half convinced that they didn't even know a world existed beyond their own narrow portion of it.

For example, she knew what Simon Bradley would think of her tiny, cluttered, bayside home because she knew exactly what her father would have thought of it—if he'd ever deigned to visit. He would have thought it too old, too small. He would have hated the bright blue walls and yellow trim in the living room. He'd have loathed the mural of the circus that decorated her bathroom wall. Mostly though, he would have seen her living there as a disgrace.

She had the distinct impression that Simon wouldn't be any different.

"Look, the reality is it doesn't matter what Nathan's father thinks of me or my house. Our only connection is the baby." As she spoke, she told her hormones to listen up. "So I'm not going to put on a show and change my life in any way to try to convince a man I don't even know that I am who I'm not."

A long second passed, then Anna laughed gently. "What does it say about me that I completely understood that?"

"That we've been friends too long?"

"Probably," Anna agreed. "Which is how I know you're making rosemary chicken tonight."

Tula smiled. Anna did know her too well. Rosemary chicken was her go-to meal when she was having company. And unless Simon was a vegetarian, everything would go great. Oh, God—what if he *was* a vegetarian? No, she thought. Men like him did lunch at steak houses with clients. "You've got me there. And once we have dinner, I'll talk to Simon about setting up a schedule for him to get to know Nathan."

"You?" Anna laughed. "A schedule?"

"I can be organized," she argued, though her words didn't carry a lot of confidence. "I just choose to not be."

"Uh-huh. How's the baby?"

Everything in Tula softened. "He's wonderful." Her gaze followed the tiny boy as he continued on his path around the kitchen, laughing and making noises as he explored his world. "Honestly, he's such a good baby. And he's so smart. This morning I asked him where his nose was and he pointed right to it."

Well, he had been waving his stuffed bunny in the air and hit himself in the face with it, but close enough.

"Harvard-bound already."

"I'll sign him up on the waiting list tomorrow," Tula agreed with a laugh. "Look, I gotta go. Get the chicken in the oven, give Nathan a bath and…ooh, maybe myself, too."

"Okay, but call me tomorrow. Let me know how it goes."

"I will." She hung up, leaned against the kitchen counter and let her gaze slide over the bright yellow kitchen. It was small but cheerful, with white cabinets, a bright blue counter and copper-bottomed pans hanging from a rack over the stove.

She loved her house. She loved her life.

And she loved that baby.

Simon Bradley was going to have to work very hard to convince her that he was worthy of being Nathan's father.

The scent of rosemary filled the little house by the bay a few hours later.

Tula danced around the kitchen to the classic rock tunes pouring from the radio on the counter and every few steps, she stopped to steal a kiss from the baby in the high chair. Nathan giggled at her, a deep, full-belly laugh that tickled at the edges of Tula's heart.

"Funny guy," she whispered, planting a kiss on top of his head and inhaling the sweet, clean scent of him. "Laughing at my dance moves isn't usually the way to my heart, you know."

He gave her another grin and kicked his fat legs in excitement.

Tula sighed and smoothed her hand across the baby's wisps of dark hair. Two weeks he'd been a part of her life and already she couldn't imagine her world without him in it. The moment she'd picked him up for the first time, Nathan had carved away a piece of her heart and she knew she'd never get it back.

Now she was supposed to hand him over to a man who would no doubt raise Nathan in the strict, rarified world in which she'd been raised. How could she stand it? How could she sentence this sweet baby to a regimented lifestyle just like the one she'd escaped?

And how could she avoid it?

She couldn't.

Which meant she had only one option. If she couldn't stop Simon from eventually having custody of Nathan—then she'd just have to find a way to loosen Simon up. She'd loosen Simon up, break him out of the world of "suits" so that he wouldn't do to Nathan what her father had tried to do to her.

Looking down into the baby's smiling eyes, she made a promise. "I'll make sure he knows how to have fun, Nathan. Don't you worry. I won't let him make you wear a toddler business suit to preschool."

The baby slapped one hand down onto a pile of dry breakfast cereal on the food tray, sending tiny O's skittering across the kitchen.

"Glad you agree," she said as she bent down, scraped them up into her hand and tossed them into the sink. Then she washed her hands and came back to the baby. "Your daddy's coming here soon, Nathan. He'll probably be crabby and stuffy, so don't let that bother you. It won't last for long. We're going to change him, little man. For his own good. Not to mention *yours*."

He grinned at her.

"Attaboy," she said and bent for another quick kiss just as the doorbell sounded. Her stomach gave a quick spin that had her taking a deep breath to try to steady it. "He's here. You're all strapped in, so you're safe. Just be good for a second and I'll go let him in."

She didn't like leaving Nathan alone in the high chair, even though he was belted in tightly. So Tula hurried across the toy-cluttered floor of her small living room and wondered how it had gotten so messy again. She'd straightened it up earlier. Then she remembered she and the baby playing after she put the chicken in the oven and—too late to worry about it now. She threw open the door and nearly gulped.

Simon was standing there, somehow taller than she remembered. He wasn't wearing a suit, either, which gave her a jolt of surprise. She got another jolt when she realized just how good he looked when he pried himself out of the sleek lines of his business "uniform." Casual in a charcoal-gray sweater, black jeans and cross trainers, he actually looked even more gorgeous, which was just disconcerting. He looked so...different. The only thing familiar about him was the scowl.

When she caught herself just staring at him like a big dummy, she said quickly, "Hi. Come on in. Baby's in the kitchen and I don't want to leave him alone, so close the door, will you, it's cold out there."

Simon opened his mouth to speak, but the damn woman was already gone. She'd left him standing on the porch and raced off before he could so much as say hello. Of course, he'd had the chance to speak, he simply hadn't. He'd been caught up in looking at her. Just as he had earlier that day in his office.

Those big blue eyes of hers were…mesmerizing somehow. Every time he looked into them, he forgot what he was thinking and lost himself for a moment or two. Not something he wanted to admit, even to himself, but there it was. Frowning, he reminded himself that he'd come to her house to set down some rules. To make sure Tula Barrons understood exactly how this bizarre situation was going to progress. Instead, he was standing on the front porch, thinking about just how good a woman could look in a pair of faded blue jeans.

Swallowing the stab of irritation at himself, he followed after her. Tula wasn't his main concern here, after all. He was here because of the child. His son? He was having a hard time believing it was possible, but he couldn't walk away from this until he knew for sure. Because if the baby was his, there was no way he would allow his child to be raised by someone else.

He'd been thinking about little else but this woman and the child she said belonged to him since she'd left his office that morning. With his concentration so unfocused, he'd finally given up on getting any work done and had gone to see his lawyer.

After that illuminating little visit, he'd spent the last couple of hours thinking back to the brief time he'd spent with Sherry Taylor. He still didn't remember much about her, but he had to admit that there was at least the possibility that her child was his.

Which was why he was here. He stepped inside and his foot came down on something that protested with a loud *squeak*. He glanced down at the rubber reindeer and shook his head as he closed the door. His gaze swept the interior of the small house and he shook his head. If more than two people were in the damn living room, they wouldn't be able to breathe at the same time. The house was old and small and…bright, he thought, giving the nearly electric blue walls an astonished glance.

The blue walls boasted dark yellow molding that ran around the circumference of the room at the ceiling. There was a short sofa and one chair drawn up in front of a hearth where a tiny blaze sputtered and spat from behind a wrought-iron screen. Toys were strewn across the floor as if a hurricane had swept through and there was a narrow staircase on the far wall leading to what he assumed was an even tinier second story.

The whole place was a dollhouse. He almost felt like Gulliver. Still frowning, he heard Tula in the kitchen, talking in a singsong voice people invariably tended to use around babies. He told himself to go on in there, but he didn't move. It was as if his feet were nailed to the wood floor. It wasn't that he was afraid of the baby or anything, but Simon knew damn well that the moment he saw the child, his world as he knew it would cease to exist.

If this baby were his son, nothing would ever be the same again.

A child's bubble of laughter erupted in the other room and Simon took a breath and held it. Something inside him tightened and he told himself to move on. To get this first meeting over so that plans could be made, strategies devised.

But he didn't move. Instead, he noticed the framed drawings and paintings on the walls, most of which were of a lop-eared bunny in different poses. Why the woman would choose to display such childish paintings was beyond him, but Tula Barrons, he was discovering, was different from any other woman he'd ever known.

The child laughed again.

Simon nodded to himself and followed the sound and the amazing scents in the air to the kitchen.

It didn't take him long.

Three long strides had him leaving the living room and entering a bright yellow room that was about the size of his walk-in closet at home. Again, he felt as out of place as a beer at a wine tasting. This whole house seemed to have been built for tiny people and a man his size was bound to feel as if he had to hunch his shoulders to keep from rapping his head on the ceiling.

He noted that the kitchen was clean but as cluttered as the living room. Canisters lined up on the counter beside a small microwave and an even smaller TV. Cupboard doors were made of glass, displaying ancient china stacked neatly. A basket with clean baby clothes waiting to be folded was standing on the table for two and the smells pouring from the oven had his mouth watering and his stomach rumbling in response.

Then his gaze dropped on Tula Barrons as she straightened up, holding the baby she'd just taken from a high chair in her arms. She settled the chubby baby on her right hip, gave Simon a brilliant smile and said, "Here he is. Your son."

Simon's gaze locked on the boy who was staring at him out of a pair of eyes too much like his own to deny. His lawyer had advised him to do nothing until a paternity test had been arranged. But Harry had always been too cautious, which was why he made such a great lawyer. Simon tended to go with his gut on big decisions and that instinct had never let him down yet.

So he'd come here mainly to see the baby for himself before arranging for the paternity test his lawyer wanted.

Because Simon had half convinced himself that there was no way this baby was his.

But one look at the boy changed all that. He was stubborn, Simon admitted silently, but he wasn't blind. The baby looked enough like him that no paternity test should be required—though he'd get one anyway. He'd been a businessman too long to do anything but follow the rules and do things in a logical, reasonable manner.

"Nathan," Tula said, glancing from the baby on her hip to Simon, "this is your daddy. Simon, meet your son."

She started toward him and Simon quickly held up one hand to keep her where she was. Tula stopped dead, gave him a quizzical look and tipped her head to one side to watch him. "What's wrong?"

What wasn't? His heart was racing, his stomach was churning. How the hell had this happened? he wondered. How had he made a child and been unaware of the boy's existence? Why had the baby's mother kept him a secret? Damn it, he had had the right to know. To be there for his son's birth. To see him draw his first breath. To watch him as he woke up to the world.

And it had all been stolen from him.

"Just…give me a minute, all right?" Simon stared at the tiny boy, trying to ignore the less-than-pleased expression on Tula Barrons's face. Didn't matter what she thought of him, did it? The important thing here was that Simon's entire world had just taken a sharp right turn.

A father.

He was a father.

Pride and something not unlike sheer panic roared

through him at a matching pace. His gaze locked on the boy, he noticed the dark brown hair, the brown eyes—exact same shade as Simon's own—and, finally, he noticed the baby's lower lip beginning to pout.

"You're making him cry." Tula jiggled the baby while patting him on the back gently.

"I'm not doing anything."

"You look angry and babies are very sensitive to moods around them," she said and soothed the boy by swaying in place and whispering softly. Keeping her voice quiet and singsongy, she snapped, "Honestly, is that scowl a permanent fixture on your face?"

"I'm not—"

"Would it physically kill you to smile at him?"

Frustrated and just a little pissed because he had to admit that she was at least partially right, Simon assumed what he hoped was a reassuring smile.

She rolled her eyes and laughed. "That's the best you've got?"

He kept his voice low, but didn't bother to hide his irritation. "You might want to back off now."

"I don't see why I should," she countered, her voice pleasant despite her words. "Sherry left *me* as guardian for Nathan and I don't like how you're treating him."

"I haven't done anything."

"Exactly," she said with a sharp nod. "You won't even let him get near you. Honestly, haven't you ever seen a child before?"

"Of course I have, I'm just—"

"Shocked? Confused? Worried?" she asked, then continued on before he could speak. "Well, imagine how Nathan must feel. His mother's gone. His home is gone.

He's in a strange place with strangers taking care of him and now there's a big mean bully glaring at him."

He stiffened. "Now just a damn min—"

"Don't swear in front of the baby."

Simon inhaled sharply and shot her a glare he usually reserved for employees he wanted to terrify into improving their work skills, fully expecting her to have the sense to back off. Naturally, she paid no attention to him.

"If you can't be nice and at least *pretend* to smile, you'll just have to go away," she said. Then she spoke to the baby. "Don't you worry, sweetie, Tula won't let the mean man get you."

"I'm not a mean—oh, for God's sake." Simon had had enough of this. He wasn't going to be chastised by anybody, least of all the short, curvy woman giving him a disgusted look.

He stalked across the small kitchen, plucked the baby from her grasp and held Nathan up to eye level. The baby's pout disappeared as if it had never been and the two of them simply stared at each other.

The baby was a solid, warm weight in his hands. Little legs pumped, arms waved and a thin line of drool dripped from his mouth when he gave his father a toothless grin. His chest tight, Simon felt the baby's heartbeat racing beneath his hands and there was a… connection that he'd never felt before. It was basic. Complete. Staggering.

In that instant—that heart-stopping, mind-numbing second—Simon was lost.

He knew it even as he stood there, beneath Tula Barrons's less than approving stare, that this was his son and he would do whatever he had to to keep him.

If this woman stood in his way, he'd roll right over her without a moment's pause. Something in his gaze must have given away his thoughts because the small blonde lifted her chin, met his eyes in a bold stare and told him silently that she wouldn't give an inch.

Fine.

She'd learn soon enough that when Simon Bradley entered a contest—he never lost.

Three

"You're holding him like he's a hand grenade about to explode," the woman said, ending their silent battle.

Despite that swift, sure connection he felt to the child in his arms, Simon wasn't certain at all that the baby wouldn't explode. Or cry. Or expel some gross fluid. "I'm being careful."

"Okay," she said and pulled out a chair to sit down.

He glanced at her, then looked back to the baby. Carefully, Simon eased down onto the other chair pulled up to the postage-stamp-sized table. It looked so narrow and fragile, he almost expected it to shatter under his weight, but it held. He felt clumsy and oversize. As if he were the only grown-up at a little girl's tea party. He had to wonder if the woman had arranged for him to feel out of place. If she was subtly trying to sabotage this first meeting.

Gently, he balanced the baby on his knee and kept one hand on the small boy's back to hold him in place. Only then did he look up at the woman sitting opposite him.

Her big eyes were fixed on him and a half smile tugged at the corner of her mouth, causing that one dimple to flash at him. She'd gone from looking at him as if he were the devil himself to an expression of amused benevolence that he didn't like any better.

"Enjoying yourself?" he asked tightly.

"Actually," she admitted, "I am."

"So happy to entertain you."

"Oh, you're really not happy," she said, her smile quickening briefly again. "But that's okay. You had me worried, I can tell you."

"Worried about what?"

"Well, how you were going to be with Nathan," she told him, leaning against the ladder back of the chair. She crossed her arms over her chest, unconsciously lifting her nicely rounded breasts. "When you first saw him, you looked…"

"Yes?" Simon glanced down when Nathan slapped both chubby fists onto the tabletop.

"…terrified," she finished.

Well, that was humiliating. And untrue, he assured himself. "I wasn't scared."

"Sure you were." She shrugged and apparently was dialing back her mistrust. "And who could blame you? You should have seen me the first time I picked him up. I was so worried about dropping him I had him in a stranglehold."

Nothing in Simon's life had terrified him like that first moment holding a son he didn't know he had. But he wasn't about to admit to that. Not to Tula Barrons at any rate.

He shifted around uncomfortably on the narrow chair. How did an adult sit on one of these things?

"Plus," she added, "you don't look like you want to bite through a brick or something anymore."

Simon sighed. "Are you always so brutally honest?"

"Usually," she said. "Saves a lot of time later, don't you think? Besides, if you lie, then you have to remember what lie you told to who and that just sounds exhausting."

Intriguing woman, he thought while his body was noticing other things about her. Like the way her dark green sweater clung to her breasts. Or how tight her faded jeans were. And the fact that she was barefoot, her toenails were a deep, sexy red and she was wearing a silver toe ring that was somehow incredibly sexy.

She was *nothing* like the kind of woman Simon was used to. The kind Simon preferred, he told himself sternly. Yet, there was something magnetic about her. *Something—*

"Are you just going to stare at me all night or were you going to speak?"

—Irritating.

"Yes, I'm going to speak," he said, annoyed to have been caught watching her so intently. "As a matter of fact, I have a lot to say."

"Good, me too!" She stood up, took the baby from him before he could even begin to protest—not that he would have—and set the small boy back in his high chair. Once she had the safety straps fastened, she shot Simon a quick smile.

"I thought we could talk while we have dinner. I made chicken and I'm a good cook."

"Another truth?"

"Try it for yourself and see."

"All right. Thank you."

"See, we're getting along great already." She moved around the kitchen with an economy of motions. Not surprising, Simon thought, since there wasn't much floor space to maneuver around.

"Tell me about yourself, Simon," she said and reached over to place some sliced bananas on the baby's food tray. Instantly, Nathan chortled, grabbed one of the pieces of fruit and squished it in his fist.

"He's not eating that," Simon pointed out while she walked over to take the roast chicken out of the oven.

"He likes playing with it."

Simon took a whiff of the tantalizing, scented steam wafting from the oven and had to force himself to say, "He shouldn't play with his food though."

She swiveled her head to look at him. "He's a baby."

"Yes, but—"

"Well, all of my cloth napkins are in the laundry and they don't make tuxedos in size six-to-nine months."

He frowned at her. She'd deliberately misinterpreted what he was saying.

"Relax, Simon. He's fine. I promise you he won't smoosh his bananas when he's in college."

She was right, of course, which he didn't really enjoy admitting. But he wasn't used to people arguing with him, either. He was more accustomed to people rushing to please him. To anticipate his every need. He was not used to being corrected and he didn't much like it.

As that thought raced through his head, he winced. God, he sounded like an arrogant prig even in his own mind.

"So, you were saying..."

"Hmm?" he asked. "What?"

"You were telling me about yourself," she prodded as she got down plates, wineglasses and then delved into a drawer for silverware. She had the table set before he gathered his thoughts again.

"What is it you want to know?"

"Well, for instance, how did you meet Nathan's mother? I mean, Sherry was my cousin and I've got to say, you're not her usual type."

"Really?" He turned on the spindly seat and looked at her. "Just what type am I then?"

"Geez, touchy," she said, her smile flashing briefly. "I only meant that you don't look like an accountant or a computer genius."

"Thanks, I think."

"Oh, I'm sure there are attractive accountants and computer wizards, but Sherry never found any." She carried a platter to the counter and began to slice the roast chicken, laying thick wedges of still-steaming meat on the flowered china. "So how did you meet?"

Simon bristled and distracted himself by pulling bits of banana out of the baby's hair. "Does it matter?"

"No," she said. "I was just curious."

"I'd rather not talk about it." He'd made a mistake that hadn't been repeated and it wasn't something he felt like sharing. Especially with *this* woman. No doubt she'd laugh or give him that sad, sympathy-filled smile again and he wasn't in the mood.

"Okay," she said, drawing that one word out into three

or four syllables. "Then how long were the two of you together?"

Irritation was still fresh enough to make his tone sharper than he'd planned. "Are you writing a book?"

She blinked at him in surprise. "No, but Sherry was my cousin, Nathan's my nephew and you're my…well, there's a relationship in there somewhere. I'm just trying to pin it down."

And he was overreacting. It had been a long time since Simon had felt off balance. But since the moment Tula had stepped into his office, nothing in his world had steadied. He watched her as she moved to the stove, scooped mashed potatoes into a bowl and then filled a smaller dish with dark green broccoli. She carried everything to the table and asked him to pour the wine.

He did, pleased at the label on the chardonnay. When they each had full glasses, he tipped his toward her. "I'm not trying to make things harder, but this has been a hell—" he caught himself and glanced at the baby "—heck of a surprise. And I don't much like surprises."

"I'm getting that," she said, reaching out to grab the jar of baby food she'd opened and left on the table. As she spooned what looked like horrific mush into Nathan's open mouth, she asked again, "So how long were you and Sherry together?"

He took a sip of wine. "Not giving up on this, are you?"

"Nope."

He had to admire her persistence, if nothing else.

"Two weeks," he admitted. "She was a nice woman but she—we—didn't work out."

Sighing, Tula nodded. "Sounds like Sherry. She never did stay with any one guy for long." Her voice softened in memory. "She was scared. Scared of making a mistake, picking the wrong man, but scared of being alone, too. She was scared—well, of pretty much everything."

That he remembered very well, too, Simon thought. Images of the woman he'd known in the past were hazy, but recollections of what he'd felt at the time were fairly clear. He remembered feeling trapped by the woman's clinginess, by her need for more than he could offer. By the damp anxiety always shining in her eyes.

Now, he felt…not guilt, precisely, but maybe regret. He'd cut her out of his life neatly, never looking back while she had gone on to carry his child and give birth. It occurred to him that he'd done the same thing with any number of women in his past. Once their time together was at an end, he presented them with a small piece of jewelry as a token and then he moved on. This was the first time that his routine had come back to bite him in the ass.

"I didn't know her well," he said when the silence became too heavy. "And I had no idea she was pregnant."

"I know that," Tula told him with a shake of her head. "Not telling you was Sherry's choice and for what it's worth, I think she was wrong."

"On that, we can agree." He took another sip of the dry white wine.

"Please," she said, motioning to the food on the table, "eat. I will, too, in between feeding the baby these carrots."

"Is that what that is?" The baby seemed to like the stuff, but as far as Simon was concerned, the practically neon orange baby food looked hideous. Didn't smell much better.

She laughed a little at the face he was making. "Yeah, I know. Looks gross, doesn't it? Once I get into the swing of having him around, though, I'm going to go for more organic stuff. Make my own baby food. Get a nice blender and then he won't have to eat this stuff anymore."

"You'll make your own?"

"Why not? I like to cook and then I can fix him fresh vegetables and meat—pretty much whatever I'm having, only mushy." She shrugged as if the extra effort she was talking about meant nothing. "Besides, have you ever read a list of ingredients on baby food jars?"

"Not recently," he said wryly.

"Well, I have. There's too much sodium for one thing. And some of the words I can't even pronounce. That can't be good for tiny babies."

All right, Simon thought, he admired that as well. She had already adapted to the baby being in her life. Something that he was going to have to work at. But he would do it. He'd never failed yet when he went after something he wanted.

He took a bite of chicken and nearly sighed aloud. So she was not only sexy and good with kids, she could cook, too.

"Good?"

Simon looked at her. "Amazing."

"Thanks!" She beamed at him, gave Nathan a few more pieces of banana and then helped herself to her own dinner. After a moment or two of companionable quiet, she asked, "So, what are we going to do about our new 'situation'?"

"I took the will to my lawyer," Simon said.

"Of course you did."

He nodded. "You're temporarily in charge..."

"Which you don't like," she added.

Simon ignored her interruption, preferring to get everything out in the open under his own terms. "Until *you* decide when and if I'm ready to take over care of Nathan."

"That's the bottom line, yes." She angled her head to look at him. "I told you this earlier today."

"The question," he continued, again ignoring her input, "is how do we reach a compromise? I need time with my son. You need the time to *observe* me with him. I live in San Francisco and have to be there for my job. You live here and—where do you work?"

"Here," she said, taking another bite and chasing it with a sip of wine. "I write books. For children."

He glanced at the rabbit-shaped salt and pepper shakers and thought about all of the framed bunnies in her living room. "Something to do with rabbits, I'm guessing."

Tula tensed, suddenly defensive. She'd heard that dismissive tone of his before. As if writing children's books was so easy anybody could do it. As if she was somehow making a living out of a cute little hobby. "As a matter of fact, yes. I write the Lonely Bunny books."

"Lonely Bunny?"

"It's a very successful series for young children." Well, she amended silently, not *very* successful. But she was gaining an audience, growing slowly but surely. And she was proud of what she did. She made children happy. How many other people could say that about their work?

"I'm sure."

"Would you like to see my fan letters? They're scrawled in crayon, so maybe they won't mean much to you. But to me they say that I'm reaching kids. That they enjoy my stories and that I make them happy." She fell back in her chair and snapped her arms across her chest in a clear signal of defense mode. "As far as I'm concerned, that makes my books a success."

One of his eyebrows lifted. "I didn't say they weren't."

No, she thought, but he had been thinking it. Hadn't she heard that tone for years from her own father? Jacob Hawthorne had cut his only daughter off without a dime five years ago, when she finally stood up to him and told him she wasn't going to get an MBA. That she was going to be a writer.

And Simon Bradley was just like her father. He wore suits and lived in a buttoned-down world where whimsy and imagination had no place. Where creativity was scorned and the nonconformist was fired.

She'd escaped that world five years ago and she had no desire to go back. And the thought of having to hand poor little Nathan off to a man who would try to regulate his life just as her father had done to her gave her cold chills. She looked at the happy, smiling baby and wondered how long it would take the suits of the world to suck his little spirit dry. The thought of that was simply appalling.

"Look, we have to work together," Simon said and she realized that he didn't sound any happier about it than she was.

"We do."

"You work at home, right?"

"Yes…"

"Fine, then. You and Nathan can move into my house in San Francisco."

"Excuse me?" Tula actually felt her jaw drop.

"It's the only way," he said simply, decisively. "I have to be in the city for my work. You can work anywhere."

"I'm so happy you think so."

He gave her a patronizing smile that made her grit her teeth to keep from saying something she would probably regret.

"Nathan and I need time together. You have to witness us together. The only reasonable solution is for you and him to move to the city."

"I can't just pick up and leave—"

"Six months," he said. He drained the last of his wine and set the empty goblet onto the table. "It won't take that long, but let's say, for argument's sake, that you move into my house for the next six months. Get Nathan settled. See that I'm going to be fine taking care of my own son, if he is my son, and then you can move back here…" He glanced around the tiny kitchen with a slow shake of his head as if he couldn't understand why anyone would willingly live there. "And we can all get on with our lives."

Damn it, Tula hadn't even considered moving. She loved her house. Loved the life she'd made for herself. Plus, she tended to avoid San Francisco like the plague.

Her father lived in the city.

Ran his empire from the very heart of it.

Heck, for all she knew, Simon Bradley and her father

were the best of friends. Now there was a horrifying thought.

"Well?"

She looked at him. Looked at Nathan. There really wasn't a choice. Tula had promised her cousin that she would be Nathan's guardian and there was no turning back from that obligation now even if she wanted to.

"Look," he said, leaning across the table to meet her eyes as though he knew that she was trying and failing to find a way out of this. "We don't have to get along. We don't even have to like each other. We just have to manage to live together for a few months."

"Wow," she murmured with a half laugh, "doesn't that sound like a good time."

"It's not about a good time, Ms. Barrons…"

"If we're going to be living together, the least you could do is call me Tula."

"Then you agree, *Tula?*"

"Do I get a choice?"

"Not really."

He was right, she told herself. There really wasn't a choice. She had to do what was best for Nathan. That meant moving to the city and finding a way to break Simon out of his rigid world. She blew out a breath and then extended her right hand across the table. "All right then. It's a deal."

"A deal," he agreed.

He took her hand in his and it was as if she'd suddenly clutched a live electrical wire. Tula almost expected to see sparks jumping up from their joined hands. She knew he felt it, too, because he released her instantly and frowned to himself.

She rubbed her fingertips together, still feeling that sizzle on her skin and told herself the next few months were going to be very interesting.

Four

Two days later, Simon swung the bat, connected with the baseball and felt the zing of contact charge up his arms. The ball sailed out into the netting strung across the back of the batting cage and he smiled in satisfaction.

"A triple at least," he announced.

"Right. You flied out to center," Mick Davis called back from the next batting cage.

Simon snorted. He knew a good hit when he saw it. He got the bat high up on his shoulder and waited for the next robotic pitch from the machine.

While he was here, Simon didn't have to think about work or business deals. The batting cages near his home were an outlet for him. He could take out his frustrations by slamming bats into baseballs and that outlet was coming in handy at the moment. While he was concentrating on fastballs, curveballs and sliders, he couldn't think about big blue eyes. A luscious mouth.

Not to mention the child who was—might be—his son.

He swung and missed, the ball crashing into the caged metal door behind him.

"I'm up two now," Mick called out with a laugh.

"Not finished yet," Simon shouted, enjoying the rush of competition. Mick had been his best friend since college. Now he was also Simon's right-hand man at the Bradley company. There was no one he trusted more.

Mick slammed a ball into the far netting and Simon grinned, then punched out one of his own. It felt good to be physical. To blank out his mind and simply enjoy the chance to hit a few balls with his friend. Here, no one cared that he was the CEO of a billion-dollar company. Here, he could just relax. Something he didn't do often. By the time their hour was up, both men were grinning and arguing over which of them had won.

"Give it up." Simon laughed. "You were outclassed."

"In your dreams." Mick handed Simon a bottle of water and after taking a long drink, he asked, "So, you want to tell me why you were swinging with such a vengeance today?"

Simon sat down on the closest bench and watched a handful of kids running to the cages. They were about nine, he guessed, with messy hair, ripped jeans and eager smiles. Something stirred inside him. One day, Nathan would be their age. He had a son. He was a father. In a few years, he'd be bringing his boy to these cages.

Shaking his head, he muttered, "You're not going to believe it."

"Try me." Mick toasted him with his own water and urged him to talk.

So Simon did. While late-afternoon sunshine slipped through the clouds and a cold sea wind whistled past, Simon talked. He told Mick about the visit from Tula. About Nathan. About all of it.

"You have a *son?*"

"Yeah," Simon said with a fast grin. "Probably. I'm getting a paternity test done."

"I'm sure you are," Mick said.

He frowned a little. "It makes sense, but yeah, looking at him, it's hard to ignore. I'm still trying to wrap my head around it myself. Hell, I don't even know what to do first."

"Bring him home?"

"Well, yeah," he said. "That's the plan. I've got crews over at the house right now, fixing up a room for him."

"And this Tula? What's she like?"

Simon pulled at his ice-cold water again, relishing the liquid as it slid down his throat to ease the sudden tightness there. How to explain Tula, he thought. Hell, where would he begin? "She's...different."

Mick laughed. "What the hell does that mean?"

"Good question," Simon muttered. His fingers played with the shrink-wrapped label on the water bottle. "She's fiercely protective of Nathan. And she's as irritating as she is gorgeous—"

"Interesting."

Simon shot him a look. "Don't even go there. I'm not interested."

"You just said she's gorgeous."

"Doesn't mean a thing," he insisted, shooting a look

at the boys as they lined up to take turns at the cages. "She's not my type."

"Good. Your type is boring."

"What?"

Mick leaned both forearms on the picnic table. "Simon, you date the *same* woman, over and over."

"What the hell are you talking about?"

"No matter how their faces change, the inner woman never does. They're all cool, quiet, refined."

Now Simon laughed. "And there's something wrong with that?"

"A little variety wouldn't kill you."

Variety. He didn't need variety. His life was fine just the way it was. If a quick image of Tula Barrons's big blue eyes and flashing dimple rose up in his mind, it was nobody's business but his own.

He'd seen close-up and personal just what happened when a man spent his time looking for *variety* instead of *sensible.* Simon's father had made everyone in the house miserable with his continuing quest for amusement. Simon wasn't interested in repeating any failing patterns.

"All I'm saying is—"

"Don't want to hear it," Simon told him before his friend could get going. "Besides, what the hell do you know about women? You're *married.*"

Mick snorted. "Last time I looked, my beautiful wife *is* a woman."

"Katie's different."

"Different from the snooty ice queens you usually date, you mean."

"How did we get onto the subject of my love life?"

"Beats the hell outta me," Mick said with a laugh.

"I just wanted to know what was bugging you and now I do. There's a new woman in your life *and* you're a father."

"Probably," Simon amended.

Mick reached out and slapped Simon's shoulder. "Congratulations, man."

Simon smiled, took another sip of water and let his new reality settle in. He was, most likely, a father. He had a son.

As for Tula Barrons being in his life, that was temporary. Strangely enough, that thought didn't have quite the appeal it should have.

"I don't know what to do about him," Tula said, taking a sip of her latte.

"What *can* you do?" Anna Hale asked from her position on the floor of the bank.

Tula looked down at the baby in his stroller and smiled as Nathan slapped his toy bunny against the tray. "Hey, do you think it's okay for the baby to be in here while you're painting? I mean, the fumes..."

"It's fine. This is just detail work," Anna said, soothing her, then she smiled. "Look at you. You're so mom-like."

"I know." Tula grinned at her. "And I really like it. Didn't think I would, you know? I mean, I always thought I'd like to have kids some day, but I never really had any idea of what it would really be like. It's exhausting. And wonderful. And..." She stopped and frowned thoughtfully. "I have to move to the city."

"It's not forever," Anna told her, pausing in laying down a soft layer of pale yellow that blended with the bottom coat of light blue to make a sun-washed sky.

"Yeah, I know," Tula said on a sigh. She walked to Anna, sat down on the floor and sat cross-legged. "But you know how I hate the idea of going back to San Francisco."

"I do," Anna said, wiping a stray lock of hair off her cheek, leaving a trace of yellow paint in her wake. "But you won't necessarily see your father. It's a big city."

Tula gave her a halfhearted grin. "Not big enough. Jacob Hawthorne throws a huge shadow."

"But you're not in that shadow anymore, remember?" Anna reached out, grabbed her hand, then winced at the yellow paint she transferred to Tula's skin. "Oops, sorry. Tula, you walked away from him. From that life. You don't owe him anything and he doesn't have the power to make you miserable anymore. You're a famous author now!"

Tula laughed, delighted at the image. She was famous in the preschool crowd. Or at least, her Lonely Bunny was a star. She was simply the writer who told his stories and drew his pictures. But, oh, how she loved going to children's bookstores to do signings. To read her books to kids clustered around her with wide eyes and innocent smiles.

Anna was right. Tula had escaped her father's narrow world and his plans for *her* life. She'd made her own way. She had a home she loved and a career she adored. Glancing at the baby boy happily gabbling to himself in his stroller, she told herself silently that she was madly in love with a drooling, nearly bald, one-foot-tall dreamboat.

What she would do when she had to say goodbye to that baby she just didn't know. But for the moment, that time was weeks, maybe months, away.

If ever she'd seen a man who wasn't prepared to be a father, it was Simon Bradley.

Instantly, an image of him popped into her brain and she almost sighed. He really was far too handsome for her peace of mind. But gorgeous or not, he was as stuffy and stern as her own father and she'd had enough of that kind of man. Besides, this wasn't about sexual attraction or the buzzing awareness, this was about Nathan and what was best for him.

So Tula would put aside her own worries and whatever tingly feelings she had for the baby's father and focus instead on taking care of the tiny boy.

She could do this. And just to make herself feel better, she mentally put her adventure into the tone of one of her books. *Lonely Bunny Goes to the City.* She smiled to herself at the thought and realized it wasn't a bad idea for her next book.

"You're absolutely right," Tula said firmly, needing to hear the confident tone in her own voice. "My father can't dictate to me anymore. And besides, it's not as if he's interested in what I'm doing or where I am."

The truth stung a bit, as it always did. Because no matter what, she wished her father were different. But wishing would never make it so.

"I'm not going to worry about running into my father," she said. "I mean, what are the actual odds of that happening anyway?"

"Good for you!" Anna said with an approving grin. Then she added, "Now, would you mind handing me the brush shaped like a fan? I need to get the lacy look on the waves."

"Right." Tula stood, looked through Anna's supplies and found the wide, white sable fan-shaped brush. She handed it over, then watched as her best friend expertly laid down white paint atop the cerulean blue ocean, creating froth on water that looked real enough Tula half expected to hear the sound of the waves.

Anna Cameron Hale was the best faux finish artist in the business. She could lay down a mural on a wall and when she was finished, it was practically alive. Just as, when this painting on the bank wall was complete, it would look like a view of the ocean on a sunny day, as seen through a columned window.

"You're completely amazing, you know that, right?" Tula said.

"Thanks." Anna didn't look back, just continued her painting. "You know, once you're settled into Simon's place, I could come up and do a mural in the baby's room."

"Oooh, great idea."

"And," Anna said coyly, turning her head to look at Tula, "it would be good practice for the nursery Sam and I are setting up."

A second ticked past. Then two. "You're—"

"I am."

"How long?"

"About three months."

"Oh my God, that's huge!" Tula dropped to her knees and swept Anna into a tight hug, then released her. "You're gonna have a baby! How'd Sam take it?"

"Like he's the first man to introduce sperm to egg!" Anna laughed again and the shine in her eyes defined just how happy she really was. "He's really excited. He called Garret in Switzerland to tell him he's going to be an uncle."

"Weird, considering you actually dated Garret for like five minutes."

"Ew." Anna grimaced and shook her head. "I don't like to think about that part," she said, laughing again. "Besides, three dates with Garret or a lifetime with his brother…no contest."

Tula had never seen her friend so happy. So content. As if everything in her world were exactly the way it was supposed to be. For one really awful moment, Tula actually felt envious of that happiness. Of the certainty in Anna's life. Of the love Sam surrounded her with. Then she deliberately put aside her own niggling twist of jealousy and focused on the important thing here. Supporting Anna as she'd always been there for Tula.

"I'm really happy for you, Anna."

"Thanks, sweetie. I know you are." She glanced at the baby boy who was watching them both through interested eyes. "And believe me, I'm glad you're getting so much hands-on experience, Aunt Tula. I don't have a clue how to take care of a baby."

"It's really simple," Tula said, following her friend's gaze to smile at the baby that had so quickly become the center of her world. "All you have to do is love them."

Her heart simply turned over in her chest. Two weeks she'd been a surrogate mom and she could hardly remember a time without Nathan. What on earth had she done with herself before having that little boy to snuggle and care for? How had she gotten through her day without the scent of baby shampoo and the soft warmth of a tiny body to hold?

And how would she ever live without it?

* * *

Simon knew how to get things done.

With Mick's assistant taking care of most of the details, within a week, Simon's house had been readied for Tula and Nathan's arrival.

He had rooms prepared, food delivered and had already lined up several interviews with a popular nanny employment agency. Tula and the baby had been in town only three days and already he had arranged for a paternity test and had pulled a few important strings so that he'd have the results a lot sooner than he normally would have.

Not that he needed legal confirmation. He had known from his first glance at the child that Nathan was his. Had felt it the moment he'd held him. Now he had to deal with the very real fact of parenthood. Though he was definitely going to go slowly in that regard until he had proof.

He'd never planned on being a father. Hell, he didn't know the first thing about parenting. And his own parent had hardly been a sterling role model.

Simon knew he could do it, though. He always found a way.

He opened his front door and accidentally kicked a toy truck. The bright yellow Dumpster was sent zooming across the parquet floor to crash into the opposite wall. He shook his head, walked to the truck and, after picking it up, headed into the living room.

Normally, he got home at five-thirty, had a quiet drink while reading the paper. The silence of the big house was a blessing after a long day filled with clients, board meetings and ringing telephones. His house had been a sanctuary, he thought wryly. But not anymore.

He glanced around the once orderly living room and blew out an exasperated breath. How could one baby have so much…stuff?

"They've only been here three days," he muttered, amazed at what the two of them had done to the dignified old Victorian.

There were diapers, bottles, toys, fresh laundry that had been folded and stacked on the coffee table. There was a walker of some sort in one corner and a discarded bunny with one droopy ear sitting in Simon's favorite chair. He stepped over a baby blanket spread across a hand-stitched throw rug and set his briefcase down beside the chair.

Picking up the bunny, he ran his fingers over the soft, slightly soggy fur. Nathan was teething, Tula had informed him only that morning. Apparently, the bunny was taking the brunt of the punishment. Shaking his head, he laughed a little, amazed anew at just how quickly a man's routine could be completely shattered.

"Simon? Is that you?"

He turned toward the sound of her voice and looked at the hall as if he could see through the walls to the kitchen at the back of the house. Something inside him tightened in expectation at the sound of Tula's voice. His body instantly went on alert, a feeling he was getting used to. In the three days she and the baby had been here, Simon had been in a near-constant state of aching need.

She was really getting to him, and the worst of it was, she wasn't even trying.

Tula was only here as Nathan's guardian. To stay until

she felt Simon was ready to be his son's father. There was nothing more between them and there couldn't be.

So why then, he asked himself, did he spend so damn much time thinking about her? She wasn't the kind of woman who usually caught his eye. But there was something about her. Something alive. Electric.

She smiled and that dimple teased him. She sang to the baby and her voice caressed him. She was here, in his house when he came home from work, and he didn't even miss the normal quiet.

He was in serious trouble.

"Simon?"

Now her voice almost sounded worried because he hadn't answered her. "Yes, it's me."

"That's good. We're in the kitchen!"

He held on to the lop-eared bunny and walked down the long hallway. The rooms were big, the wood gleaming from polish and care and the walls were painted in a warm palate of blues and greens. He knew every creak of the floor, every sigh of the wind against the windows. He'd grown up in this house and had taken it over when his father died a few years ago.

Of course, Simon had put his own stamp on the place. He'd ripped up carpeting that had hidden the tongue-and-groove flooring. He'd had wallpaper removed and had restored crown moldings and the natural wood in the built-in china cabinets and bookcases.

He'd made it his own, determined to wipe out old memories and build new ones.

Now he was sharing it with the son he still could hardly believe was his.

Stepping into the kitchen, he was surrounded by the scented steam lifting off a pot of chili on the stove. At the table, Tula sat cross-legged on a chair while spooning something green and mushy into Nathan's mouth.

"What is that?" he asked.

"Hi! What? Oh, green beans. We went shopping today, didn't we, Nathan?" She gave the boy another spoonful. "We bought a blender and some fresh vegetables and then we came home and cooked them up for dinner, didn't we?"

Simon could have sworn the infant was listening to everything Tula had to say. Maybe it was her way of practically singing her words to him. Or maybe it was the warmth of her tone and the smile on her face that caught the baby's attention.

Much as it had done for the boy's father.

"It's so cold outside, I made chili for us," she said, tossing him a quick grin over her shoulder.

The impact of that smile shook him right down to the bone.

Mick had been right, he thought. Tula was nothing like the cool, controlled beauties he was used to dating.

And he had to wonder if she was as warm in bed as she was out of it.

"Smells good," he managed to say.

"Tastes even better," she promised. "Why don't you come over here and finish feeding Nathan? I'll get dinner for us."

"Okay." He approached her and the baby cautiously and wanted to kick himself for it. Simon Bradley had a reputation for storming into a situation and taking charge. He could feed a baby for God's sake. How difficult could it be?

He took Tula's chair, picked up the bowl of green

bean mush and filled a spoon. Behind him, he could sense Tula's gaze on him, watching. Well, he'd prove not only to himself, but to her, that he was perfectly capable of feeding a baby.

Spooning the green slop into Nathan's mouth, he was completely unprepared when the baby spat it back at him. "What?"

Tula's delighted laughter spilled out around him as Simon wiped green beans from his face. Then she leaned in, kissed him on the cheek and said, "Welcome to fatherhood."

An instant later, her smile died as he looked at her through dark eyes blazing with heat. Her mouth went dry and a sizzle of something dark and dangerous went off inside her.

They stared at each other for what felt like forever until finally Simon said, "That wasn't much of a kiss. We'll have to do better next time."

Next time?

Five

Tula remembered sitting in her own kitchen thinking that this was not a good idea. Now she was convinced.

Yet here she was, living in a Victorian mansion in the city with a man she wasn't sure she liked—but she really did want.

Last night at dinner, Simon had looked so darn cute with green beans on his face that she hadn't been able to stop herself from giving in to the impulse to kiss him. Sure, it was just a quick peck on his cheek. But when he'd turned those dark brown eyes on her and she'd read the barely banked passion there, it had shaken her.

Not like she was some shy, retiring virgin or anything. She wasn't. She'd had a boyfriend in college and another one just a year or so ago. But Simon was nothing like them. In retrospect, they had been boys and Simon was all man.

"Oh God, stop it," she told herself. It wouldn't do any good of course. She'd been indulging in not so idle daydreams centered on Simon Bradley for days now. When she was sleeping, her brain picked up on the subconscious thread and really went to town.

But a woman couldn't be blamed for what she dreamed of when she slept, right?

"It's ridiculous," she said, tugging at her desk to move it into position beneath one of the many mullioned windows. A stray beam of rare January sunlight speared through the clouds and lay across her desktop. She didn't take the time to admire it though, instead, she went back to getting the rest of her temporary office the way she wanted it.

She didn't need much, really. Just her laptop, a drawing table where she could work on the illustrations for her books and a comfy chair where she could sit and think.

"Hmm. If you don't need much stuff, Tula, why is there so much junk in here?" A question for the ages, she thought. She didn't *try* to collect things. It just sort of…happened. And being here in the Victorian where everything had a tidy spot to belong to made her feel like a pack rat.

There were boxes and books and empty shelves waiting to be filled. There were loose manuscript pages and pens and paints and, oh, way too many things to try to organize.

"Settling in?"

She jumped about a foot and spun around, holding one hand to her chest as if trying to keep her heart where it belonged. He stood in the open doorway, a half smile on his handsome face as if he knew darn well that he'd scared about ten years off her life.

Giving Simon a pained glare, she snapped, "Wear a bell or something, okay? I about had a heart attack."

"I do live here," Simon reminded her.

"Yeah, I know." As if she could forget. She'd lain awake in her bed half the night, imagining Simon in his bed just down the hall from her. She never should have kissed him. Never should have breached the tense, polite wall they'd erected between them at their first meeting.

Only that morning, they'd had breakfast together. The three of them sitting cozily in a kitchen three times the size of her own. She had watched Simon feeding a squirming baby oatmeal while dodging the occasional splat of rejected offerings and darned if he hadn't looked…cute doing it.

She groaned inwardly and warned herself again to get a grip. This wasn't about playing house with Simon.

He strolled into her office with a look of stunned amazement on his face. "How do you work in this confusion?"

She'd just been thinking basically the same thing, but she wasn't about to give him the satisfaction of knowing it. "An organized mind is a boring mind."

One dark eyebrow lifted and she noticed he did that a lot when they were talking. Sardonic? Or just irritated?

"You paint, too?" he asked, nodding at the drawing table set up beneath one of the tall windows.

"Draw, really. Just sketches," she said. "I do the illustrations for my books."

"Impressive," he said, moving closer for a better look.

Tula steeled herself against what he might say once he'd had a chance to really study her drawings. Her father had never given her a compliment, she thought. But in the end that hadn't mattered, since she drew her pictures for the children who loved her books. Tula knew she had talent, but she had never fooled herself into believing that she was a great artist.

He thumbed through the sketch papers on the table and she knew what he was seeing. The sketches of Lonely Bunny and the animals who shared his world.

His gaze moving to hers, he said softly, "You're very good. You get a lot of emotion into these drawings."

"Thank you." Surprised but pleased, she smiled at him and felt warmth spill through her when he returned that smile.

"Nathan has a stuffed rabbit. But he needs a new one. The one he has looks a little worse for wear."

She shook her head sadly, because clearly he didn't know how much a worn, beloved toy could mean to a child. "You never read *The Velveteen Rabbit?*" she asked. "Being loved is what makes a toy real. And when you're real, you're a little haggard looking."

"I guess you're right." He laughed quietly and nodded as he looked back at her sketches. "How did you come up with this? The Lonely Bunny, I mean."

Veering away from the personal and back into safe conversation, she thought, oddly disappointed that the brief moment of closeness was already over.

Still, she grinned as she said, "People always ask writers where they get their ideas. I usually say I find my ideas on the bottom shelf of the housewares department in the local market."

One corner of his mouth quirked up. "Clever. But not really an answer, either."

"No," she admitted, wrapping her arms around her middle. "It's not."

He turned around to face her and his warm brown eyes went soft and curious. "Will you tell me?"

She met his gaze and felt the conversation drifting back into the intimate again. But she saw something in his eyes that told her he was actually interested. And until that moment, no one but Anna had ever really cared.

Walking toward him, she picked up one of the sketches off the drawing table and studied her own handiwork. The Lonely Bunny looked back at her with his wide, limpid eyes and sadly hopeful expression. Tula smiled down at the bunny who had come along at just the right time in her life.

"I used to draw him when I was a little girl," she said more to herself than to him. She ran one finger across the pale gray color of his fur and the crooked bend of his ear. "When Mom and I moved to Crystal Bay, there were some wild rabbits living in the park behind our house."

Beside her, she felt him step closer. Felt him watching her. But she was lost in her own memories now and staring back into her past.

"One of the rabbits was different. He had one droopy ear, and he was always by himself," she said, smiling to herself at the image of a young Tula trying to tempt a wild rabbit closer by holding out a carrot. "It looked to me like he didn't have any friends. The other rabbits stayed away from him and I sort of felt that we were two of a kind. I was new in town and didn't have any friends, so I made it my mission to make that bunny like me. But no matter how I tried, I couldn't get him to play with me.

"And believe me, I tried. Every day for a month. Then one day I went to the park and the other rabbits were there, but Lonely Bunny wasn't." She stroked her fingertip across her sketch of that long-ago bunny. "I looked all over for him, but couldn't find him."

She stopped and looked up into eyes filled with understanding and compassion and she felt her own eyes burn with the sting of unexpected tears. The only person she had ever told about that bunny was Anna. She'd always felt just a little silly for caring so much. For missing that rabbit so badly when she couldn't find him.

"I never saw him again. I kept looking, though. For a week, I scoured that park," she mused. "Under every bush, behind every rock. I looked everywhere. Finally, a week later, I was so worried about him, I told my mother and asked her to help me look for him."

"Did she?" His voice was quiet, as if he was trying to keep from shattering whatever spell was spinning out around them.

"No," she said with a sigh. "She told me he had probably been hit by a car."

"What?" Simon sounded horrified. "She said *what?*"

Tula choked out a laugh. "Thanks for the outrage on my behalf, but it was a long time ago. Besides, I didn't believe her. I told myself that he had found a lady bunny and had moved away with her."

She set the drawings down onto the table and turned

to him, tucking her hands into her jeans pockets. "When I decided to write children's books, I brought Lonely Bunny back. He's been good for me."

Nodding, Simon reached out and tapped his finger against one of her earrings, setting it into swing. "I think you were good for him, too. I bet he's still telling his grandbunnies stories about the little girl who loved him."

Her breath caught around a knot of tenderness in the middle of her throat. "You surprise me sometimes, Simon."

"It's only fair," he said. "You surprise me all the damn time."

Seconds ticked past, each of them looking at the other as if for the first time. Simon was the first to speak and when he did, it was clear that the moment they had shared was over. At least for now.

"Do you have everything you need?"

"Yes." She took a breath and an emotional step back. "I just need to move my chair into place and—"

"Where do you want it?"

She looked up at him. He was just home from work, so he was wearing a dark blue suit and the only sign of relaxation was the loosening of the knot in his red silk tie.

"You don't have to—"

He shrugged out of his suit jacket. His tailored, long-sleeved white shirt clung to a truly impressively broad chest. She swallowed hard as she watched him grab hold of the chair and she wondered why simply taking off his suit jacket in front of her seemed such an intimate act.

Maybe, she thought, it was because the suit was who he was. And laying it aside, even momentarily, felt like an important step.

As soon as that thought entered her mind, Tula pushed it away.

Nothing intimate going on here at all, she reminded herself. Just a guy, helping her move a chair. And she'd do well to keep that in mind. Anything else would just be asking for trouble.

"Over there," she said, pointing to the far corner.

"You want to move that box out of the way?"

She did, pushing the heavy box of books with her foot until Simon had a clear path. He muscled the oversize chair across the room, then angled it in a way so that she'd be facing both windows when she sat in it.

"How's that?"

"Perfect, thanks."

He looked around the room again. "Where's the baby?"

"In his room. He took a late nap today."

"Right." He wandered around the room now, peeking into boxes, glancing at the haphazard stacks of papers on her desk. "You know, I've got some colored file folders in my office you could use."

She bristled. "I have my own system."

Simon looked at her and lifted that eyebrow again. "Chaos is a system?"

"It's only chaos if you can't find your way around. I can."

"If you say so." He moved closer. "Is there anything else I can do?"

"Um, no thanks," Tula whispered, feeling the heat of him reach for her. This was her fault, she told herself as tension in the room began to grow. If she hadn't given him that impulsive kiss, they'd still be at odds. If she hadn't opened herself up, causing him to be so darn sweet, they wouldn't be experiencing this closeness now.

So she spoke up fast, before whatever was happening between them could go any further. "Why don't you go check on Nathan while I finish up in here? I've still got a lot of unpacking to do."

She stepped past him and dug into a carton of books, deliberately keeping her back to him. Her heart was pounding and her stomach was spinning with a wild blend of nerves and anticipation. Pulling out a few of the books, she set them on the top shelf and let her fingertips linger on the bindings.

But Simon didn't leave. Instead, he went down on one knee beside her, cupped her chin and turned her face toward him.

"I don't know what's going on between us any more than you do. But you can't avoid me forever, Tula. We're living together, after all."

"We're living in the same house, that's all," she corrected breathlessly. "Not together."

"Semantics," he mused, a half smile tugging at one corner of his mouth.

Oh, she knew what he was thinking because she was thinking the same thing. Well, actually, there was very little *thinking* going on. This was more feeling. Wanting. Needing.

She shook her head. "Simon, you know it would be a bad idea."

"What?" he asked innocently. "A kiss?"

"You're not talking about just a kiss."

"Rather not talk at all," he admitted, his gaze dropping to her mouth.

Tula licked her lips and took a breath that caught in her lungs when she saw his eyes flash. "Simon…"

"You started this," he said, leaning in.

"I know," she answered and tipped her head to one side as she moved to meet him.

"I'll finish it."

"Stop talking," she told him just before his mouth closed over hers.

Heat exploded between them.

Tula had never known anything like it before. His mouth took hers hungrily, his tongue parting her lips, sweeping inside to claim all of her. He pulled her tightly against him until they were both kneeling on the soft, plush carpet. His hands slid up and down her back, dipping to cup the curve of her behind and pull her more tightly against him.

Tula felt the rock-hard proof of just how much Simon wanted her and that need echoed inside her. Her mind blanked out and she gave herself up to the river of sensations he was causing. She tangled her tongue with his, leaning into him, wrapping her arms around his neck and holding on as if she were afraid of sliding off the edge of the world.

He tore his mouth from hers, buried his face in the curve of her neck and whispered, "I've been thinking about doing this, about *you,* ever since you first walked into my office."

"Me, too," she murmured, tipping her head to give him better access. Her body was electrified. Every cell was buzzing, and at the core of her she burned and ached for him.

He dropped his hands to the hem of her sweater and slid his palms beneath the heavy knit material to slide across her skin. She felt the burn of his fingers, the sizzle and pop in her bloodstream as he stoked flames already burning too brightly.

Oh, it had been way too long since anyone had touched her, Tula thought, letting her head fall back on a soft sigh. And she'd *never* been touched like this before.

"Let me," he murmured, drawing her sweater up and off, baring breasts hidden beneath a bra of sheer, pink lace.

Cool air caressed her skin in a counterpoint to the heat Simon was creating. One corner of her mind was shrieking at her to stop this while she still could. But the rest of her was telling that small, insistent voice to shut up and go away.

"Lovely," he said, skimming the backs of his fingers across her nipples.

She shivered when his thumbs moved over the tips of her hardened nipples, the brush of the lace intensifying his touch to an almost excruciating level of excitement. Tula trembled as he unhooked the front clasp of her bra and sucked in a quick breath when he pushed the lacy panel aside and cupped her breasts in his hands.

He bent his head to take first one nipple and then the other into his mouth and Tula swayed in place. Threading her fingers through his thick hair, she held him to her and concentrated solely on the feel of his lips and tongue against her skin.

She wanted him naked, her hands on his body. She wanted to lie back and pull him atop her. She wanted to feel their bodies sliding together, to look up into his eyes as he took her to—

An insistent howl shattered the spell between them.

Simon pulled back from her and whipped his head around to stare at the doorway. "What was that?"

"The baby." Still trembling, Tula grabbed the edges of her bra and hooked it together. Then she reached for her sweater and had it back on in a couple of seconds. "I've got the baby monitor in here so I could hear him while I worked."

She waved one hand at what looked like a space-age communication device and Simon nodded. "Right. The monitor."

Scrambling to her feet, Tula backed away from him quickly.

"Don't do that," Simon said, standing up and reaching for her. "I can see in your eyes that you're already pretending that didn't happen."

"No, I'm not," she assured him, though her voice was as shaky as the rest of her. Pushing one hand through the short, choppy layers of her hair, she blew out a breath and admitted, "But I should."

"Why?" He winced when the baby's cries continued, but didn't let go of her.

Tula shook her head and pulled free of his grasp. "Because this is just one more complication, Simon. One neither one of us should want."

"Yeah," he said, gaze meeting hers. "But we do."

"You can't always have what you want," she countered, taking a step back, closer to the open doorway. "Now I really have to go to the baby."

"Okay. But Tula," he said, stopping her as she started to leave. "You should know that I *always* get what I want."

When Tula carried Nathan into her office half an hour later, she found a stack of colored file folders lying on top of her desk. There was a brief note. "Chaos can be controlled. S."

"As if I didn't know who put them there," she told the baby. "He had to put his initial on the note?"

She set the baby down on a blanket surrounded by toys, then took a seat at her desk. Her fingertips tapped against the file folders until she finally shrugged and opened one.

"I suppose it couldn't hurt to try a little filing, right?"

Nathan didn't have an opinion. He was far too fascinated by the foam truck with bright red headlights he had gripped in his tiny fists.

Tula smiled at him, then set to work straightening up her desk. It went faster than she would have thought and though she hated to admit it, there was something satisfying about filing papers neatly and tucking them away in a cabinet. By the time she was finished, her desktop was cleared off for the first time in…ever.

Her phone rang just as she was getting up to take the baby downstairs for his dinner. "Hello?"

"Tula, hi, this is Tracy."

Her editor's voice was, as always, friendly and businesslike. "Hi, what's up?"

"I just need you to give me the front matter for the next book. Production needs it by tomorrow."

"Right." For one awful moment, Tula couldn't remember where she'd put the letter to her readers that always went in the front of her new books. She liked adding that extra personal touch to the children who read her stories.

The scattered feeling was a familiar one. Despite what she had bragged to Simon about knowing where everything was, she usually experienced a moment of sheer panic when her editor called needing something. Because she knew that she would have to stall her while she located whatever was needed.

"It's okay, Tula," Tracy said as if knowing exactly what she was thinking. "I don't need it this minute and I know it'll take you some time to find it. If you just email the letter to me first thing in the morning, I'll hand it in."

"No, it's okay," Tula said suddenly as she realized that she had just spent hours filing things away neatly. "I actually know right where it is."

"You're kidding."

Laughing, she reached out, opened the once-empty file cabinet and pulled out the blue folder. *Blue for Bunny Letters,* she thought with an inner smile. She even had a system now. Sure, she wasn't certain how long it would last, but the fun of surprising her editor had been worth the extra work.

"Poor Tracy," Tula said with sympathy. "You've been putting up with my disorganization for too long, haven't you?"

"You're organized," Tracy defended her. "Just in your own way."

She appreciated the support, but Tula knew very well that Tracy would have preferred just a touch more organizational effort on her writer's part. "Well, I'm trying something new. I am holding in my hand an actual file folder!"

"Amazing," Tracy said with a chuckle. "An organized writer. I didn't know that was possible. Can you fax the letter to me?"

"I can. You'll have it in a few minutes."

"Well, I don't know what inspired the new outlook, but thanks!"

Once she hung up, Tula faxed in the letter, then filed it again and slipped the folder back into the cabinet with a rush of pride. Wouldn't Simon love to know that he'd been right? As for her, she'd managed to straighten up a mess without losing her identity.

Grinning down at the baby, she asked, "What do you think, Nathan? Can a person have chaos *and* control?"

She was still wondering about that when she carried the baby downstairs to the kitchen.

A few hours later, Tula said sharply, "You have to make sure he doesn't slip."

"Well," Simon assured her, "I actually knew that much on my own."

He was bent over the tub, one hand on Nathan's narrow back while he used his free hand to move a soapy washcloth over the baby's skin. "How is it you're supposed to hold him and wash him at the same time?"

Tula grinned and Simon felt a hard punch to his chest. When she really smiled it was enough to make him want to toss her onto the nearest flat surface and bury himself inside her heat.

The kiss they'd shared only a couple of hours before was still burning through him.

He still had the taste of her in his mouth. Had the feel of her soft, sleek skin on his fingers.

Now, as she leaned over beside him to slide a wet washcloth over Nathan's head, he inhaled and drew her light, floral scent into his lungs. He must have let a groan slip from his throat because she stopped, leaned back and looked up at him.

"Are you okay?"

"Not really," he said tightly, focusing now on the baby who was slapping the water with both hands and chortling over the splashes he made.

"Simon—"

"Forget it, Tula. Let's just concentrate on surviving bath time, okay?"

She sat back on her heels and looked up at him. "Now who's pretending it didn't happen?"

He laughed—a short, sharp sound. "Trust me when I say that's not what I'm doing."

"Then why—"

Giving her a hard look, he said, "Unless you're willing to finish what we started, drop it, Tula."

She snapped her mouth closed and nodded. "Right. Then I'll just go get Nathan's jammies ready while you finish. Are you good on your own?"

Good question.

He always had been.

Before.

Now he wasn't so sure.

"We'll be fine. Just go."

She scooted out of the bathroom a moment later and Nathan drew his first easy breath since bath time had started. He looked down into the baby's eyes and said, "Remember this, Nathan. Women are nothing but trouble."

The tiny boy laughed and slapped the water hard enough to send a small wave into his father's face.

"Traitor," Simon whispered.

Six

A few nights later, Simon had had enough of slipping through his own house like a damn ghost. Ever since the kiss he had shared with Tula, he'd kept his distance, staying away not only from her, but from the baby as well. He wondered where in the hell the paternity test results were and asked himself how he was supposed to keep his mind on anything else when memories of a too brief kiss kept intruding.

Hell, it wasn't just the kiss. It was Tula herself and that was an irritation he hadn't expected. She was in his mind all the time. Moving through his thoughts like a shadow, never really leaving, always haunting.

She walked into the room and he felt a hard slam of desire pulse through him. His body was hard and his hands itched to touch her. But she seemed blissfully unaware of what she was doing to him, so damned if he'd let her know.

"Maybe we should talk about how this is going to work," he said when Tula walked into the living room.

Lamplight shone on her blond hair and glittered in her eyes so that it almost looked as if stars were in their depths, winking at him. She was nothing like the women he was usually drawn to. And she was everything he wanted. God, knowing that she was there, in his house, right down the hall from his own bedroom, was making for some long, sleepless nights.

Oblivious of his thoughts, she smiled at him, crossed the room and dropped into a wingback chair on his right. Curling her feet up beneath her, she said, "Yes, the baby went right to sleep as soon as I laid him down. Thanks for asking."

He frowned to himself and silently admitted that, no, he hadn't been thinking about the baby. Hardly his fault when she was so near. He dared any man to be able to keep his mind off Tula Barrons for long. "I assumed he was sleeping since he's not with you and I can't hear him crying."

She studied him for a thoughtful moment. "Don't you think you should start being a part of the whole putting-Nathan-to-bed routine?"

"When I get the results of the paternity test, I will."

Until then, he was going to hang back. Taking part in bath time a few nights ago had taught him that he was too damn vulnerable where that baby was concerned. He had actually thought of himself as the boy's father.

What if he found out Nathan wasn't his?

No, better to protect himself until he knew for sure.

"Simon, Nathan is your son and pretending he isn't won't change that."

"That's what we need to talk about," he said, standing

to walk to the wet bar across the room. "Do you want a drink?"

"White wine if you've got it."

"I do." He took care of the drinks then sat down again opposite her. Outside, night was crouched at the glass. A fire burned in the hearth and the snap and hiss of the flames was the only sound for a few minutes. Naturally, Tula couldn't keep quiet for long.

"Okay, what did you want to talk about?"

"This," he said, sweeping one hand out as if to encompass the house and everything in it.

"Well, that narrows it down," Tula mused, taking a sip of wine. "Look, I get that you're a little freaked by the whole 'instant parenthood' thing, but we can't change that, right?"

"I didn't say—"

"And I've closed up my house and moved here to help you settle in—"

"Yes, but—"

"You'll get to know the baby. I'll help as much as I can, but a lot of this is going to come down on you. He's your son."

"We don't know that for sure yet and I think—"

She ran right over him again and Simon was beginning to think that he'd never get the chance to have any input in this conversation. Normally, when he spoke, people listened. No one interrupted him. No one talked over him. Except Tula. And as annoying as it was to admit, even to himself, he liked that about her. She wasn't hesitant. Not afraid to stand up for herself or Nathan. And not the least bit concerned about telling him exactly what she thought.

Still, he was forced to grind his teeth and fight for patience as she continued.

She waved her glass of wine and sloshed a bit onto her denim-covered leg. She hardly noticed.

"So basically," she said, "I'm thinking a man like you would feel better with a clear-cut schedule."

That got his attention. "A man like *me?*"

She smiled, damn it and his temperature climbed a bit in response.

"Come on, Simon," she teased. "We both know that you've got a set routine in your life and the baby and I have disrupted it."

This conversation was not going the way he'd planned. He was supposed to be the one taking charge. Telling Tula how things would go from here. Instead, the tiny woman had taken the reins from his hands without him even noticing. Simon took a sip of the aged scotch and let the liquor burn its way down his throat. It sat like a ball of fire in the pit of his stomach and he welcomed the heat. He looked at Tula, watching him with good humor sparkling in her eyes and not a trace of the sexual pull he'd been battling for days.

Irritating as hell that she could so blithely ignore what had been driving him slowly insane. Fresh annoyance spiked at having her so calmly staring him down, pretending to know him and his life and not even once allowing that there was something between them.

Plus, in a few well-chosen words, Tula had managed to both insult and intrigue him.

"I don't have a routine," he grumbled, resenting the hell out of the fact that she had made him sound like a doddering old man concentrating solely on his comfortable rut in life.

She laughed and the sound filled the big room with a warmth it had never known.

"Simon, I've only been in this house a handful of days and I already know your routine as well as you do. Up at six, breakfast at seven," she began, ticking items off on her fingers. "Morning news at seven-thirty, leave for the office at eight. Home by five-thirty..."

He scowled at her, furious that she was reducing his life to a handful of statistics. And even more furious that she was right. How in the hell had that happened? Yes, he preferred order in his life, but there was a distinct difference between a well-laid-out schedule and a monotonous habit.

"A drink and the evening news at six," she went on, still smiling as if she was really enjoying herself, "dinner at six-thirty, work in your study until eight..."

Dear God, he thought in disgust, had he really become so trapped in his own well-worn patterns he hadn't even noticed? If he was this transparent to a woman who had known him little more than a week, what must he look like to those who knew him well? Was he truly that *predictable?* Was he nothing more than an echo of his own habits?

That thought was damned disconcerting.

"Don't stop now," he urged before taking another sip of scotch. "You're on a roll."

"Well, there my tale ends," she admitted. "By eight I'm putting the baby to bed and I have no idea what you do with the rest of your night." She leaned one elbow on the arm of the chair and grinned at him. "Care to enlighten me?"

Oh, he'd like to enlighten her. He'd like to tell her she was wrong about him entirely. Unfortunately, she wasn't. He'd like to take her upstairs and shake up *both* of their routines. But he wasn't going to. Not yet.

"I don't think so," he said tightly, still coming to grips with his own slide into predictability. "Besides, I didn't want to talk about me. We were going to talk about the baby."

"For us to talk about the baby," she countered with a satisfied nod, "you would have to actually spend time with him. Which you manage to avoid with amazing regularity."

"I'm not avoiding him."

"It's a big house, Simon, but it's not that big."

He stood up, suddenly needing to move. Pace. Something. Sitting in a chair while she watched him with barely concealed disappointment was annoying.

Simon knew he shouldn't care what she thought of him, but damned if he wanted her thinking he was some sort of coward, hiding from his responsibilities. *Or* an old man stuck in a routine of his own devising. He walked to the wide bay window with a view of the park directly across the street. Moonlight played on the swing sets and slides, illuminating the playground with a soft light that looked almost otherworldly.

"I haven't gotten the paternity test results back yet," he said, never taking his gaze from the window and the night beyond the glass.

"You know he's yours, Simon. You can feel it."

He looked down at her as she walked up beside him. "What I feel isn't important."

"That's where you're wrong, Simon," she said sadly, looking up at him. "In the end, what you feel is the *only* important thing."

He didn't agree. Feelings got in the way of logical

thought. And logic was the only way to live your life. He had learned that lesson early and well. Hadn't he watched his own father, Jarod Bradley, nearly wipe out the family dynasty by being so chaotic, so disordered and flighty that he neglected everything that was important?

Well, Simon had made a pledge to himself long ago that he was going to be nothing like his father. He ran his world on common sense. On competency. He didn't trust "feelings" to get him through his life. He trusted his mind. His sense of responsibility and order.

Which was how he'd slipped into that rut he was cursing only moments ago. His father hadn't had a routine for anything. He'd greeted each day not knowing what was going to happen next. Simon preferred knowing exactly what his world was doing—and arranging it to suit himself when possible.

Besides, despite what Tula thought, he wasn't so much actively avoiding Nathan as he had been avoiding *her.* Ever since that kiss. Ever since he'd held her breasts cupped in his hands he hadn't been able to think of anything else but getting his hands on her again. And until he figured out exactly what that would mean, he was going to keep right on avoiding her.

Damn it, things used to be simple. He saw an attractive woman, he talked her into his bed. Now, Tula was all wrapped up in a tight knot with the child who was probably his son and Simon was walking a fine line. If he seduced her and then dropped her, couldn't she make it more difficult for him to get custody of Nathan? And what if he had sex with her and didn't *want* to let her go? What then?

There was no room in his life for a woman as flighty

and unorganized as she was. She thrived in chaos. He needed order.

They were a match made in hell.

"Are you even listening to me?"

"Yes," he muttered, though he was actually trying to *not* listen to her.

Which was no more successful than trying not to think about her.

Tula wasn't comfortable in the city.

Ridiculous, of course, since she'd spent so much of her childhood there. Her parents separated when she was only five and her mother, Katherine, had moved them to Crystal Bay. Close enough that Tula could see her father and far enough away that her mother wouldn't have to.

Crystal Bay would always be home to Tula. Right from the first, she'd felt as though she belonged there. Life was simpler, there were no piano lessons and tutors. Instead, there was the local public school where she'd first met Anna Cameron. That friendship had really helped shape who she was. The connection with Anna and her oh-so-normal family had helped her gain the self-confidence to eventually face down her father and refuse to fall in line with his plans for her life.

Now being in San Francisco only reminded her of those long, lonely weekends with her father. Not that Jacob Hawthorne was evil, he simply hadn't been interested in a daughter when he'd wanted a son. And the fact that his daughter didn't care at all about business was another big black mark against her.

Funny, Tula thought, she had long ago gotten past the regrets she had for how her relationship with her father had died away. Apparently though, there was still a tiny spark inside her that wished things had been different.

"It's okay though," she said aloud to the baby who wasn't listening and couldn't have cared less. "I'm doing fine, aren't I, Nathan? And you like me, right?"

If he could speak, she was sure Nathan would have agreed with her and that was good enough for now.

She sighed and pushed the stroller along the sidewalk. Nathan was bundled up as if they were exploring the Arctic Circle, but the wind was cold off the bay and the dark clouds hanging over the city threatened rain.

She and the baby had been in that house for days and it was harder and harder to be there without thoughts of Simon filling her mind. She knew it was pointless, of course. She and Simon had nothing in common except that flash of heat that had practically melded them together during that amazing kiss.

But she couldn't help where her mind went. And lately, her mind kept slipping into wildly inappropriate thoughts of Simon. Which was exactly why she had bundled Nathan up for a walk. She needed to clear her head. Needed to get back to work on the book that was due by the end of the month. It was hard enough eking out the time for illustrations and storyboards while the baby was napping. Forcing herself to work on the Lonely Bunny's antics while daydreaming about Simon made it nearly impossible.

Whenever Tula was having a hard work day, she would take a walk, just to feel the bite of the fresh air, see people, listen to the world outside her own mind. Ideas didn't pop into an idle mind. They had to be fostered, engendered. And that usually meant getting out into the world.

Actually, one of her most popular books had been born at the grocery store in Crystal Bay. She remembered watching a pallet of vegetables being delivered and immediately, she'd felt that magic "click" in her brain that told her an idea was forming. Soon, she'd had the story line for *Lonely Bunny Visits the Market.*

"So see, Nathan, we're actually working!" She chuckled a little and picked up the pace.

There were so many people scurrying along the sidewalks, Tula felt lost. But then she'd been feeling a little lost since settling into Simon Bradley's house. She hadn't written a word in three days and even her illustrations were being ignored. She couldn't keep this up much longer. She had deadlines to meet and editors to appease.

And Simon was taking up so many of her thoughts, she was afraid she wouldn't be able to think of anything else.

The only bright side was that she knew Simon was feeling just as frustrated as she was. That he wanted her as much as she did him. And she couldn't help relishing that sweet rush of completely feminine power that had filled her when he'd practically thrown her out of the bathroom during Nathan's bath time a few days ago. He hadn't trusted himself around her.

Which was just delicious, she thought. Of course it would be crazy to surrender to whatever it was that was simmering between them. She had Nathan to think about, after all. She couldn't just give in to what she was feeling and not think about the consequences.

Don't I sound responsible? she thought with surprise.

Well, she was. Now. Now that she had Nathan in her

life, she had to judge every decision she made along the measurement of what was good for him. And sleeping with his father couldn't be a good idea. Especially knowing that it was up to *her* to decide when Simon was ready for custody.

She stopped short.

Was that why he had kissed her?

Was he trying to seduce her into giving him Nathan?

"Now, that's a horrible thought," she said aloud.

"I beg your pardon?"

"Hmm?" Tula looked at the older woman who had stopped on the sidewalk to look at her. "Oh, sorry. I was actually talking to myself."

"I see." The woman's eyes went wide and she hurried past.

Tula laughed a little, then stepped to the front of the stroller to check on Nathan. "Well, sweetie, I think that nice lady thought I was crazy."

He kicked his legs, waved his arms and grinned at her. All the approval she needed, Tula thought, and stepped around to push him along the sidewalk again.

There were stores, of course. Small boutiques, coffee bars and even a cozy Italian restaurant with tables grouped together on the sidewalk.

But what caught her eye was the bookstore.

"Let's go see, Nathan."

She stepped inside and paused long enough to enjoy the atmosphere. An entire store devoted to books and the people who loved them. Was there anything better? Crossing to the children's section, Tula smiled at the parents indulging their kids by sitting on the brightly colored rugs to pick out books.

When she saw a little girl reading *Lonely Bunny Makes a Friend* Tula's heart swelled with pride.

She wandered over to the shelf where her books were lined up and, taking a pen from her purse, began signing the copies there.

A few minutes later, a voice stopped her mid-scrawl.

"Excuse me."

Tula looked at a woman in her mid-forties with a name tag that read Barbara and smiled. "Hi."

The woman looked her up and down, taking in her faded jeans, blue suede boots and windblown hair before asking, "What are you doing?"

Tula dug into her purse and pulled a roll of gold-and-black autographed copy stickers that she always carried with her. "I'm the author and I thought since I was here I would just sign your stock, if that's all right."

She had never had trouble before. Usually bookstores liked having signed copies of the books on the shelves to help with sales.

"You're Tula Barrons?" Barbara asked with a wide grin. "That's wonderful! My daughter loves your books and I can tell you they sell very well for us here in the store."

"I'm always glad to hear that," Tula said and hurried her signature as Nathan started to fuss.

"You live locally?" Barbara asked.

"Temporarily," Tula told her and felt a slight wince inside at the admission. She didn't know how long she would be staying in the city, but she was already dreading having to leave both Nathan and Simon.

"Would you be interested in doing a signing here at the store?" the woman asked. "We could set it up for you to do a reading at the same time. I think the kids would love it."

"Uh," Tula hedged, not sure if she should agree or not. Normally, she would have, of course. But now that she had Nathan to worry about...

"Please consider it," Barbara urged, looking around the children's area at the brightly colored floor rugs, the tiny tables and chairs. "I know most authors hate doing signings, but I can promise you a success! Your books are very popular here and I know the children would get a big kick out of meeting the woman who writes the Lonely Bunny stories."

Tula followed her gaze and looked at the dozen or so kids sprinkled around the area, each of them lost in the wonders of a book. Yes, her life was a little up in the air at the moment, but a couple hours of her time wasn't that much of a sacrifice, was it?

"I'd love to," she finally said.

"That's *great,*" Barbara replied. "If you'll just give me a number where I can reach you, we'll set something up. How does three weeks sound?"

"It's fine," Tula told her. While Barbara went to get a pad and pen to take down her information, Tula told herself that in three weeks, she might be back living in Crystal Bay. Alone. That would mean a drive into the city for the signing, but if she was gone from Simon's life, she would at least be able to stop in and see Nathan while she was here.

Her heart ached at the thought. That baby had become so much a part of her life and world already, she couldn't even imagine being nothing more than a casual visitor to him. She put the signed book back on the shelf, walked to the front of the stroller and went down to her knees.

Running her fingers across the baby's soft cheek, she looked into brown eyes so much like his father's it was eerie and said, "What will I do without you, Nathan? If I lose you now, you won't even remember me, will you?"

He laughed and kicked his legs, turning his head this way and that, taking in all the primary colors and the bright lights.

Her already aching heart began to tear into pieces as she realized that Nathan would never know how much she loved him. Or how much it hurt to think of not being a part of his life.

She'd agreed to be the baby's guardian for her cousin Sherry's sake. But Tula had had no idea then that doing the right thing was going to one day destroy her.

Simon got home early the following day and no one was there to appreciate it.

Damned if he'd be so boring that Tula could set her watch—if she had the organizational skills to wear one—by him. He was still fuming over her monologue the night before, ticking off his daily routine and making him sound as exciting as a moldy rock.

In response, Simon had been shaking up his routine all day long. He had gone through the flagship of the Bradley department stores, stopping to chat with clerks. He'd personally talked to the managers of the departments, instead of sending Mick to do it. He had even helped out in the stockroom, walking a new employee through the inventory process.

His employees had been surprised at his personal

interest in what was happening with the store. But he had also noted that everyone he talked with that day was pleased that he'd taken the extra time to listen to them. To really pay attention to what was happening.

Simon couldn't imagine why he hadn't done it years ago. He was so accustomed to running his empire from the sanctity of his office, he'd nearly forgotten about the thousands of employees who depended on him.

Of course, Mick had ribbed him about his sudden aversion to routine.

"This new outlook on life wouldn't have anything to do with a certain children's book author, would it?"

Simon glared at him. "Butt out."

"Ha! It does." Mick followed him out the door and down the hall to the elevator. "What did she say that got to you?"

He was just aggravated enough by what Tula had had to say the night before that he told Mick everything. He finished by saying, "She ticked off my day hour by hour, on her fingers, damn it."

Mick laughed as the elevator doors swept closed and Simon stabbed the button for the ground floor of the department store. "Wish I'd seen your face."

"Thanks for the support."

"Well come on, Simon," Mick said, still chuckling. "You've got to admit you've dug yourself a pretty deep rut over the years."

"There's nothing wrong with a tight schedule."

Mick leaned against the wall. "As long as you allow yourself some room to breathe."

"You're on her side?"

Grinning, Mick said, "Absolutely."

Grumbling under his breath at the memory, Simon

stalked up the stairs, haunted by the now unnatural silence. For years, he'd come home to the quiet and had relished it. Now after only a few days of having Tula and the baby in residence…the silence was claustrophobic. Made him feel as if the walls were closing in on him.

"Ridiculous. Just enjoy the quiet while you've got it," he muttered. At the head of the stairs, he headed down the hall toward his room, but paused in front of the nursery. The baby wasn't there, but the echo of him remained in the smell of powder and some indefinable scent that was pure baby.

He stepped inside and let his gaze slide across the stacked shelves filled with neatly arranged diapers, toys and stuffed animals. He smiled to himself and inspected the closet as well. Inside hung shirts and jackets, clustered by color. Tiny shoes were lined up like toy soldiers on the floor below.

In the dresser, he knew he would find pajamas, shorts, pants, socks and extra bedding. A colorful quilt lay across the end of the crib and a small set of bookshelves boasted alphabetically arranged children's books.

Tula might thrive in chaos herself, he mused, but here in the baby's room, peace reigned. Everything was tidy. Everything was calm and safe and…perfect. He'd had a crew in to paint the room a neutral beige with cream-colored trim, but Tula had pronounced it too boring to spark the baby's inner creativity. It hadn't taken her long to have pictures of unicorns and rainbows on the walls, or to hang a mobile of primary-colored stars and planets over the crib.

Shaking his head, Simon sat down in the cushioned rocker and idly reached to pull one of the books off the shelves. *Lonely Bunny Finds a Garden.*

"Lonely Bunny," he read aloud with a sigh. Now that he'd heard her story, he could imagine Tula as a lonely little girl with wide blue eyes, trying to make friends with a solitary rabbit. He frowned, thinking about how her mother had so callously treated her daughter's fears.

He was feeling for Tula. Too much.

Opening the book, Simon read the copyright page and stopped. Her name was listed as Tula Barrons Hawthorne.

He frowned as his memory clicked into high gear, shuffling back to when he was dating Nathan's mother, Sherry. He remembered now. She had been living here in the city then and she'd told him that her uncle was in the same business as Simon.

"Jacob Hawthorne." Simon inhaled slowly, deeply, and felt old anger churn in the pit of his stomach.

Jacob Hawthorne had been a thorn in his side for years. The man's chain of discount department stores was forever vying for space that Simon wanted for his own company. Just three years ago, Jacob had cheated Simon out of a piece of prime property in the city that Simon had planned to use for expansion of his flagship store.

That maneuver had cost Simon months in terms of finding another suitable property for expansion.

Not to mention the fact that Jacob had bought up several of the Bradley department stores when Simon's father was busily running the company into the ground. The old man had taken advantage of a bad situation and made it worse. Hell, he'd nearly succeeded in getting his hands on the Bradley *home.*

By the time Simon had taken over the family business, it was in such bad shape he'd spent years rebuilding.

Jacob Hawthorne was ruthless. The old pirate ran his company like a feudal lord and didn't care who he had to steamroll to get his own way.

At the time Simon had briefly dated Sherry, he'd enjoyed the thought of romancing a member of Hawthorne's family, knowing the old coot would have been furious if he'd known. But Sherry's own clingy instability had ended the relationship quickly. Now, though, he had a son with the woman—which made his child a relative of Jacob Hawthorne.

There was a bitter pill to choke down. And he figured it would be even harder for the old pirate to swallow it. But there was more, too. If Sherry and Tula were cousins, then Tula was also a relative of Jacob Hawthorne. Interesting. But before his thoughts could go any further, his cell phone rang.

"Bradley."

"Simon, it's Dave over at the lab."

He tensed. This was the call he'd been waiting for for days. The results of the paternity test were in. He would finally know for sure, one way or the other.

"And?" he asked, not wanting to waste a moment on small talk when something momentous was about to happen.

"Congratulations," his old friend said, a smile in his tone. "You're a father."

Everything in Simon went still.

There was a sense of rightness settling over him even as an unexpected set of nerves shook through him. He was a father. Nathan was really his.

"You're sure?" he asked, moving his gaze around the

room, seeing it now with fresh eyes. His *son* lived here. "No mistakes?"

"Trust me on this. I ran the test twice myself. Just to be sure. The baby's yours."

"Thanks, Dave," he said, tossing the book onto the nearby tabletop and standing up. "I appreciate it."

"No problem."

When his friend hung up, Simon just stared down at his phone. *No problem?*

Oh, he could think of a few.

Such as what to do about the woman who was making him insane. The very woman who stood between him and custody of *his* son.

Seven

Tula knew something was different, she just couldn't put her finger on what it was exactly. Ever since she and Nathan had returned from their walk, Simon had been…watching her. Not that he hadn't looked at her before, but there was something more in his gaze now. Something hungry, yet wary.

There was a strained sense of anticipation hanging over the beautiful house that only added to the anxiety she had been feeling for days. She was on edge. As though there were tightened wires inside her getting ready to snap.

Just being around Simon was difficult now. As it had been ever since that kiss. He made her want too much. Need too much. And now, with those dark eyes locked on her and heat practically rolling off of him in waves, she could hardly draw a breath.

She made it through dinner and through Nathan's bath time and was about to read the baby his nightly story. Oh, she knew the baby didn't understand the words or what the stories meant, but she enjoyed the quiet time with him and felt that Nathan liked hearing the soft soothing tones of her voice as he fell asleep. Before she could begin, Simon walked into the nursery.

Tula smiled in spite of the coiled, unspoken strain between them. For the first time, he was inviting himself to Nathan's nightly ritual. "Hi."

"I thought I'd join you tonight." Simon looked at her for a long moment, then shifted his gaze to the tiny boy in the crib. Slowly, he walked across the floor and Tula sensed that she was witnessing something profound. Simon's features were taut, his eyes unreadable. There was a careful solicitude in his attitude she'd never seen before.

Leaning over the crib, Simon looked down at the boy in the pale blue footed jammies as if really seeing him for the first time.

"Simon?" she asked quietly, as if hesitant to break whatever spell was spinning out into the room. "What is it? You've been weird all night. Is something wrong?"

He shifted a quick look at her before turning his gaze back on Nathan. The baby stared up at him, then rubbed his eyes and sighed sleepily.

"Wrong?" Simon echoed in a thick hush of sound. "No. Nothing's wrong. Everything's right. I got the paternity test results this afternoon."

She sucked in a breath of air. Of course, from the beginning, she had known that Simon was Nathan's father. Sherry wouldn't have lied about something like that. But Tula could understand that Simon, a demon for rules and order and logic, would have to wait to be convinced.

"And?" she prompted.

"He's my son." Three words, spoken with a sort of dazed wonder that sent a flutter of something warm racing along her spine.

He reached into the crib and cupped one side of Nathan's face in the palm of his hand. The baby smiled up at him and Simon's eyes went soft, molten with emotions too deep to speak. Tula watched it all and felt her own heart melt as a man recognized his son for the very first time.

Seconds ticked past and still it was as if the world had taken a breath and held it. As if the planet had stopped spinning and the population of the earth had been reduced to just the three of them.

This small moment was somehow so intense, so important, that the longer it went on the more Tula felt like an outsider. An intruder on a private scene. That thought hurt far more than she would have thought it could.

For weeks now, she alone had been the baby's entire universe. When she was forced to share Nathan with Simon, she was still the central figure because Nathan's father was, if nothing else, a stubborn man. Determined to hold himself emotionally apart even while making room in his life for the boy. Now she saw that Simon had accepted the truth. He knew Nathan was his and he would be determined to have his son for himself.

As it should be, Tula reminded herself, despite the pain ratcheting up in the center of her chest. This was what Sherry had wanted—that Nathan would know his father. That Simon and his son would make a family.

A family, she told herself sadly, of *two*.

With that thought echoing over and over through her mind, Tula stepped back from the crib, intending to leave the two of them alone. But Simon reached out and grabbed her arm, pulling her to a stop.

"Don't go."

She looked up at him. The room was dark but for the night-light that projected constellations of stars onto the ceiling. In the dim glow of those stars, she watched his eyes and shook her head. "Simon, you should have a minute alone with Nathan. It's okay."

"Stay, Tula." His voice was low, hardly more than a dark rumble of sound.

"Simon…"

He pulled her closer until he could wrap one arm around her shoulders. Then he turned her toward the crib and they both looked down at the boy who had fallen asleep. There would be no story tonight. Nathan's tiny features were perfect, the picture of innocence. His small hands were flung up over his head, his fingers curling and relaxing as if in his dreams he was playing catch with the angels.

"He's beautiful," Simon whispered.

Tula's throat tightened even further. It was a miracle, she thought, that she could even breathe past the hard knot of emotion clogging her throat. "Yes, he is."

"I knew he was mine, right from the first," he admitted. "But I had to be sure."

"I know."

He turned his head to look down at her. Emotions charged his eyes with sparks that dazzled her. "I want my son, Tula."

"Of course you do." Her heart cracked a little further.

He would have Nathan and she would have...Lonely Bunny.

"I want you, too," he admitted.

"What?" Jolted out of her private misery, she could only stare up into brown eyes that shimmered with banked heat. This she hadn't seen coming. She hadn't expected. Something inside her woke up and shivered. Was he saying...

"Now," he said, drawing her from the room into the hall, leaving the sleeping infant laying beneath his night-light of floating stars.

"Simon—"

"I want you now, Tula," he repeated, drawing her close, framing her face with his hands.

Ah, she thought. He wanted Nathan forever. He wanted her *now.* That was the difference. She chided herself silently for even considering that he might have meant something different. A twist of regret grabbed at her but she relentlessly pushed it aside.

She'd been in his home for nearly a week. She knew Simon Bradley was a cool, calm man who didn't make decisions lightly. He liked to think he responded to his gut instincts, but the truth was, he looked at a situation from every angle before making a decision.

He wasn't the kind of man who would take some sexual heat and a shared love for a child and build it into some crazy happily-ever-after scenario. That was all in her mind.

And her heart.

She should have known better. *How silly,* she told herself, staring up into his eyes. How foolish she'd been to allow herself to care for him. To idly spin daydreams that had never had a chance to come true.

The three of them weren't a family. They were a temporary unit. Until Simon and Nathan had found their way together. Then good old "Aunt Tula" would go home and maybe come to the city once in a while for a visit.

As Nathan got older, he would no doubt resent time spent with her as simply time lost with his friends. He would be awkward with her, she thought, her heart breaking at the realization. Kind to a distant relative when his father forced him to be polite.

The little boy she loved so much wouldn't remember her love or the comfort he had derived from it. How she had sung to him at night and played peekaboo in the mornings. He wouldn't know that she would have done anything for him. Wouldn't recall that they had once been as close as mother and son.

He would have no memories of these days and nights, but they would haunt *her* forever.

She would be alone again. But this time, it would be so much worse. Because this time, she would know exactly what she was missing.

"Tula," Simon whispered, drawing her back from thoughts that were threatening to drown her in misery. He tipped her face up until their gazes were locked, his searching, hers glittering with a sheen of tears she refused to shed for the death of a dream that should never have been born.

So very foolish, she thought now, looking up at Simon Bradley. Until this very moment, Tula hadn't had any idea that she was more than halfway in love with a man she would never have.

"What is it?" he demanded. "Are you crying?"

"No," she said quickly because she couldn't let him

know that she had just said goodbye to a fantasy of her own making. "Of course not."

He accepted her word for that as his thumbs traced over her cheekbones.

"Come to my room with me, Tula," he said softly, his voice an erotic invitation she knew she couldn't resist. More, she knew she didn't want to resist it. She'd let the fantasy go but she would be a fool to turn her back on the reality, however brief it might be.

Reaching up, she covered his hands with her own and gave him the answer they both needed. "Yes, Simon. I'll come with you. I want you, too. Very much."

"Thank God." He bent and kissed her, hard and fast.

"Just let me turn the monitor on first," she said, walking back into the nursery, shooting a quick look at the baby as he sighed and smiled through his dreams. She flipped the switch on the monitor, knowing the receivers in hers and Simon's rooms would pick up every breath the baby made during the night.

She stared down at Nathan for a long moment, then turned her gaze on the doorway. There Simon stood, dark eyes burning with a fire that thrummed inside her just as hotly. Her body ached, her core went damp with need. She moved toward him and as she stepped into the hallway, he pulled her in close, then swung her up into his arms.

"I can walk, you know," she said wryly, the last of her sorrow draining away against a tide of rising passion. In spite of her protest, she secretly delighted in being carried against his hard, strong body.

"But why walk when you can ride?" One of his eyebrows lifted into the arch that she knew so well and she had to admit that being snuggled against Simon's broad chest was much preferable to a long walk down a silent hall.

The house sighed like a tired old woman settling down for a good night's rest. The creaks and groans of the wood were familiar to her now and Tula felt as though she were wrapped in warmth.

Warmth that suddenly enveloped her in heat as Simon dipped his head to claim another brief, fierce kiss. When he broke the kiss, his dark eyes were flashing with something that sent a quick chill racing along Tula's spine. Passion and just a hint of something more dangerous shone down at her and Tula's stomach erupted with a swarm of what felt like bees.

Head spinning, heart pounding, she linked her arms around his neck as he strode into his bedroom and headed for the wide, quilt-covered bed. She had never been in his room before and she glanced around at the huge space. Wildly masculine, the room was done in brown and dark blue. Deep brown leather chairs were drawn up in front of a blazing tiled fireplace. Twin bay windows overlooked the street, the park beyond and the distant ocean. The bed was big enough, she thought wryly, to sleep four comfortably and moonlight poured through the windows to lay in a silver path along the mattress. As if someone, somewhere, had drawn them a road map to where they both wanted to go.

"Gotta have you. Now," he muttered thickly, dropping her to the bed and following after.

"Yes, Simon," she answered, reaching for the buttons on his shirt, tearing at them when they refused to give.

Simon was half-crazed with wanting her. Everything

he had planned to say to her tonight dried up in the face of the overwhelming need clutching at him. Pulling at the hem of her bloodred sweater, he dragged it up and over her head to display the silky pink camisole she wore beneath. His gaze locked on her pebbled nipples. No bra. That was good. Less time wasted.

Simon hadn't been able to keep his mind on anything but Tula for hours. The question of his son's parentage had been answered and any other damn questions could just wait their turn. This was what he needed. What he had to have. Her.

Just her.

He pulled the camisole up, exposing her breasts to his hungry gaze and his mouth watered for a taste of her. He shrugged out of his shirt as she pushed the material down his arms, but beyond that, he couldn't be bothered.

Clothes would come off when they needed to. For now...he bent his head to her breasts and took first one nipple, then the other into his mouth. She gasped and arched off the bed, pushing herself into him, silently begging for more.

He gave her what she wanted.

Lips, tongue, teeth ran across the pink, sensitized tips of her breasts. Her taste filled him, her sighs inflamed him. Her fingers threaded through his hair, holding him to her breast as she squirmed under him, desperate for more. For everything.

He knew that feeling and shared it. His body ached. He was so hard for her he felt as though he might combust if he didn't get inside her. Tearing his mouth from her breasts, he worked his way down her incredibly lush body.

"So small, so perfect," he whispered, his breath hot against her skin.

"I'm not small," she countered, then gasped when his tongue traced a line around her belly button. "You're just abnormally tall."

He grinned and glanced up at her.

She shrugged. "Fine. I'm short."

"And curvy," he added, flicking the snap of her jeans and drawing down the zipper in one smooth move. His fingertips slid across her skin and she whimpered.

Simon smiled again and tugged at the jeans keeping him from her. They slid off her legs and fell to the floor. He paused then to admire the scrap of pink lace that made up the thong she wore. "If I'd known those jeans were hiding something like this, we'd have made it here long before now."

She ran her tongue across her bottom lip and everything in Simon fisted.

"Now that you know," she teased, "what are you planning on doing about it?"

In answer, he tugged the lace down her legs and off, shifted position and pulled her to the edge of the bed.

"Thought I'd start with this," he said and ran his tongue across the most sensitive spot on her body.

She jolted and instinctively squirmed beneath his strong hands holding her in place. But Simon wasn't letting her go anywhere. Instead, he pulled her closer to him, draped her legs across his shoulders and took her core with his mouth.

Tula groaned helplessly against the onslaught of emotions, sensations rampaging through her system. She looked down the length of her own body to watch him as he kissed her more intimately than anyone ever had before.

It was erotic. Sensuality personified, to see him licking her, tasting her and at the same time to feel what he was making her feel. Spirals of need and want clung together inside her and twisted into a frantic knot that seemed to pulse along with the beat of her heart.

And as her heartbeat quickened so did the tension coiling inside her. Tighter, faster, she felt herself nearing a precipice that swept higher with every passing moment. She raced toward it, surrendering to the incredible sensations coursing through her. She held nothing back—sighing, groaning, whispering his name as he pushed her further along the twisting road to completion.

Her breath was strangled in her lungs. She reached for the explosion she knew was coming and when the end came, her hands clenched the quilt beneath her and Tula held on as if for her life. The world rocked and her mind simply shut down under the onslaught of too many tiny shuddering ripples of pleasure.

Even before the last rolling sigh of satisfaction had settled inside her, Simon was there, moving her on the mattress, levering himself over her.

Staring down into her eyes, he entered her and Tula gasped at yet one more sensation. One more amazing invasion of her heart and mind and body. She held on to his shoulders and looked into dark brown eyes that were shadowed with secrets and shining with the same overpowering passion that held her in its grip. Again and again, his body claimed hers in the most intimate way possible. Again and again, she gave herself up to him, holding nothing back. Again and again, he pushed her higher and faster than she'd ever gone before.

The mind-numbing, soul-shattering climax, when it rushed through her, was enough to steal what little breath she had left. Moments later, she felt his release pound through him and heard him groaning her name. Then he collapsed atop her, his breath wheezing from his lungs, his heartbeat hammering in his chest.

Tula wrapped her arms around him and held him close, not wanting him to move yet. Not wanting to let go of the closeness that was somehow even more intimate than what they had just shared.

What could have been minutes or hours passed in a sensual haze of completion. Finally, he lifted his head, met her gaze and gave her a smile that at once made him look sexy and playful. That one smile slipped inside her and gave her the last nudge she needed to take the slippery slide into something she feared was probably, heaven help her, *love.*

"What is it?" he asked, voice quiet. "You look worried."

She was. Worried for her own sanity. Her own well-being. Falling in love with Simon would be a huge mistake, Tula thought grimly, so she just wouldn't do it. She would refuse to take that last step. It wouldn't be easy, she knew, but protecting herself was too important. Instinctively she realized she needed protection, too. Because loving and *losing* Simon would be enough to devastate her.

"Worried?" she echoed lamely, scrambling for something to say.

"I used protection," he assured her. "You weren't really paying attention, but I did."

"Oh. Thanks," she said, though a part of her wondered if it might not have been better if he hadn't. Then she would have had a chance at having a baby of her own. A child that would help fill the hole that losing Nathan was going to dig in her heart.

"Tula—" He pushed himself up on his elbows, took a breath and said, "We should talk about what just happened."

"Do we have to?" she asked, hating for this time to end with what couldn't possibly be good news. Whenever a man told a woman they had to talk, it was rarely to say, "Boy, that was great, I'm really happy."

He rolled to one side, and the chill in the room settled over her skin the moment he left her. He stacked pillows against the headboard and leaned back, his gaze on her. "Yeah. We do. Look, this was…inevitable, I think."

"Like death and taxes you mean?" she muttered, already hating how this conversation was going.

"You know what I'm talking about."

"Yeah, I do. And you're right," she sighed in agreement and sat up beside him on the bed.

He was sprawled naked, completely at ease. But Tula was suddenly feeling a little fragile. A little exposed. So she grabbed the edge of the quilt and tossed it over her, covering herself from breasts to knees. "Simon, you don't have to feel guilty or make a speech. I wanted this, too. You didn't seduce me into anything."

"I know."

"Well," she said with a small, self-conscious laugh. "Thanks for noticing."

"Not the point, Tula," he said. "The point is, we're still involved over Nathan and I want to make sure we understand each other."

She turned her head to look at him. "What are you talking about?"

Frowning, he pushed one hand through his hair. "Just that, you hold the strings when it comes to Nathan's custody."

She nodded, unable to look away from his eyes, once so warm and now looking as cold as the damp winter night outside. Somehow, he had taken a step away from her without actually leaving her side. Amazing that he could pull that off naked, but he managed.

"I don't want this," he continued, voice hard and flat, "what just happened here between us, to affect that."

Stunned, Tula could only stare at him, dumbfounded. This was not what she had been expecting. She'd thought that he was about to deliver the old, that-was-a-mistake-that-won't-be-repeated speech. Instead, he was intimating… *"What?"*

His mouth flattened into a grim line and that one eyebrow lifted. Surprisingly, she found it far less charming this time.

"Are you serious?" she demanded, indignant fury driving her words. "You really think I'm the kind of person who would use *this* against you somehow?"

"I didn't say that."

"Oh, yes you did," she told him, tossing the quilt aside and scooting off the bed. She grabbed her jeans and pulled them on over bare skin when she couldn't spot her lace thong. "I can't believe this. After what we just did, you could think that I, how could you think that? Amazing. And I'm so stupid. I should have seen this coming."

"Just wait a damn minute—"

She glanced at him over her shoulder. "That is about the most insulting thing anyone's ever said to me."

"I wasn't trying to insult you."

"So it's just a bonus then."

He climbed off the bed and went to grab his own jeans. Tugging them on, he said in a patient, calm tone that made her want to throw something, "Tula, you're overreacting. We're two adults, we should be able to talk about this without getting emotional."

"Emotional? Oh, could I show you emotional. Right now I want to throw something at that swelled head of yours."

"Not helpful," he pointed out, then looked around as if judging what she might grab and hurl at him.

"There's one of the differences between us, Simon," she snapped, whipping her head around to glare at him as she grabbed up her sweater. "Throwing things sounds very helpful to me right now. See, I'm not *afraid* to get emotional."

"What the hell are you talking about?" Now it was his turn to look insulted. "Who said I was afraid? This isn't even about fear."

"Really? Looks that way to me. My God, Simon." She cocked her head and narrowed her eyes on him. Shaking her head, she said, "You relaxed for like what? Twenty minutes? Was I on your schedule? Did you pencil me in—*Sex with Tula*—then back to business?"

"Don't be ridiculous," he muttered.

"Oh, now I'm ridiculous," she echoed, tossing both hands high then letting them fall. "You're the one making this into something it never was. This little speech you're making isn't about Nathan at all. It's about you backing away from allowing yourself to feel something genuine."

"Please." He scoffed at her and that one eyebrow winged up. "This isn't about feelings, Tula. We both had an itch and we scratched it. That's all."

She hissed in a breath and her eyes narrowed even farther until the slits were so tiny it was practically a miracle she could see him at all. "An *itch?* That's what you call what just happened?"

"What do you call it?" he asked.

Good question. She wasn't about to call it anything nice *now.* She wouldn't give him the satisfaction. So instead, she ignored the subject entirely. "Honestly, Simon, the very minute you felt close to me at all, you pulled back and hid behind that stiff, businessman persona you wear as if it were just another three-piece suit."

"Excuse me?"

"Oh," she said, warming to her theme and riding on bruised feelings and insult, "I'm just getting started. You're worried that now that I've been in the fabulous Simon Bradley's bed I might try to use that in deciding Nathan's future? Well, trust me when I say that sex with you won't sway my decision about you taking custody..."

He folded his arms over his chest. "Was there an insult in there?"

"Quite possibly, but I wasn't finished."

"Finish then. I knew there was more coming."

"You haven't proved to me yet that you're anywhere near ready to take care of a baby. Heck, until you were absolutely sure he was your son, you hardly went near him."

"And that's bad?"

"It is when you're too busy protecting yourself to give a child a chance."

"That's not what I was doing."

They stared at each other, gazes simmering with passions that had nothing to do with sex.

"This was clearly a mistake," Tula said a moment later, when she thought she could speak without shrieking. "But thankfully it's one that doesn't have to be repeated."

"Right. Probably best." Simon shoved one hand through his hair and said, "I still want you."

Tula looked at him for a long moment before admitting, "Yeah. Me, too. Good night, Simon."

She left the room and he didn't stop her. But she couldn't help turning back for one last look as she walked out. He looked powerful. Sexy.

Very alone.

And even after everything that had just happened, something inside her urged Tula to go back to him. Wrap her arms around him and hold on.

She had to remind herself that he had *chosen* solitude.

Eight

"I handled it badly, I know that."

"Yeah," Mick agreed cheerfully the following day. "That about covers it. Were you *trying* to piss her off?"

"No," Simon said, shaking his head as he thought about the night before. Hell, he couldn't remember much besides the urgent need he had felt to get her under him. Although the fight afterward was etched clearly enough in his mind. He still wasn't sure how it had happened. He hadn't meant to alert her to the fact that he was aware of the power she held in the situation. Hadn't meant to throw down a gauntlet just so that she could hit him over the head with it.

All he had really wanted to do was let her know that he wasn't going to be led around by his groin. That he was more than his passions. That sex with her, no matter how astounding, wasn't going to change him.

Simon made the rules.

Always.

But somehow, when he was around Tula, rational thought went out the window. Today, here in his office, away from the woman who was making him crazed, he was able to think more clearly. Now what he needed to know was what exactly Mick had found out about Tula Barrons Hawthorne.

"Never fight with a woman after sex," Mick was telling him. "They're feeling all warm and cozy and whatever. Men want to sleep. So hell, even *talking* after sex can be dangerous—if you ever want sex again."

Oh, he did, Simon thought. He wanted her the moment she left his room. He had wanted her all night and had awakened that morning aching for her. *Want* wasn't the issue.

"Just skip the advice and tell me what information you turned up."

Mick frowned at him and Simon thought that this was the downside of having your best friend work for you. He was less likely to take orders well and more likely to deliver his opinion whether Simon wanted it or not. "What did you find out? I know she's related to Jacob Hawthorne, but how? Niece?"

"A lot closer than that, as it turns out. She's his daughter."

"His what?" Simon went on alert. "His *daughter?*"

His mind raced as he listened to Mick give him more details.

"Hawthorne and his ex split when Tula was a kid. Mom moved with her to Crystal Bay. Tula visited her father often, but several years ago, she appears to have cut all ties with people here completely—including her father. My source didn't know much about it, just that Tula's a sore spot with the old man."

He had already known about her moving to that little town with her mother, Simon thought. But why would she cut all ties with everyone here, including her father? And why had he never heard about a daughter before? Was the old bastard protecting his child? Simon wouldn't have thought Jacob Hawthorne capable of familial loyalty.

"And," Mick added, "seems that when she started publishing children's books, she began using her middle name, Barrons. It's a family name, after her maternal grandmother. That grandmother left a will that provided a trust for Tula so that she—"

He straightened up in his desk chair and leaned both forearms on the neatly stacked files on his desk. "How big a trust?"

Mick thumbed through the papers he held. "To you, fairly small. To most of the world, very nice. It at least allowed her to buy her house and support herself while writing."

"Her books don't earn much?"

Mick shook his head. "She has a small, but growing readership for her Lonely Bunny series. The money will probably improve, but between her writing and the trust, she gets along and lives well within her limited means."

"Interesting." Her father was rich and she lived in a tiny house nearly an hour away from the city. What was the story behind that? he wondered.

"She hasn't seen her father in a few years that I can

find," Mick continued. "But then, the old man almost never leaves the city, either."

Hell, Simon thought, Jacob hardly left the Hawthorne building. He had a penthouse suite at the top of the structure that was his company's headquarters. He ruled his world from the top of his tower and rarely interacted with the "little people."

But as he thought that, Simon had to wince. Until the other day when he had deliberately gone through the store chatting with his employees, people could have said the same thing about him. There were some very uncomfortable similarities between Simon and his enemy.

"Is there anything else?" he asked, mainly to get his mind off that realization.

"No," Mick said, laying the sheaf of papers on his lap. "I can probably get more if you want me to dig deeper."

He thought about that for a moment. If he turned Mick loose and told him to dig, he'd have every piece of information available on Tula Barrons within a couple of days. But did he need more? He now knew who she was. He knew that she was the daughter of his enemy.

That was plenty.

While Mick talked, offering advice that he wasn't listening to, Simon tried to consider the situation objectively. He was attracted to Tula, obviously. The passions she stirred in him were like nothing he'd ever known. But now he knew who she was and damned if he could bring himself to trust a Hawthorne. So where did that leave him?

"What're you planning?"

He glanced at Mick. "I don't know what you're talking about."

"Right. I've seen that look before," his friend said, settling into the chair in front of Simon's desk. "Usually just before you're plotting some major takeover of an unsuspecting CEO."

Simon laughed and missed his point deliberately. "No CEO is ever unsuspecting."

"Damn it, Simon, what're you up to?"

"The less you know, the better off you are," he said, knowing that his friend would try to argue him out of the plan quickly forming in his mind.

"You mean the less you have to listen to my objections."

"That, too."

Mick slapped one hand down hard on the arm of his chair. "You're crazy, you know that? So what if she's a Hawthorne? Her father's a miserable old goat. She's got nothing to do with him."

"Doesn't matter."

"Damn it, Simon," Mick continued. "She split with him years ago. Doesn't even use her real name for God's sake."

"She's still his daughter," Simon insisted. "Don't you get it? The daughter of the man who tried to destroy my family is now in *charge* of when I get custody of my own son. How the hell am I supposed to take that, Mick? What if she just decides to never approve my custody of Nathan?"

"You really think she'd do that?"

"She's a Hawthorne." As far as he was concerned, that explained everything. God, he was an idiot. He had actually begun to trust Tula. He'd *felt* for her. More than he had anyone else in his life. Now he finds out this? For all he knew, Jacob had manufactured Nathan's mother's will. Maybe he and his daughter were in this together. Conspiring to dangle his son in front of him only to snatch him back.

He sprang to his feet as if the thought of sitting still another moment was going to kill him. Turning his back on his friend, he stared out the wide window at the view of San Francisco that Tula had admired so the first day he met her.

But instead of the high-rises and the glittering bay beyond the city, he saw *her.*

Her eyes. Her smile. That damn dimple in her cheek. He heard her sigh, felt the ripples of satisfaction rolling through her body as they took each other.

It had been one night since he had been with her and he wanted her again so badly, it was gnawing at him. Had she planned that, too? Had she deliberately set out to seduce him just so she could crush him later and sit with her father to enjoy the show?

His guts tightened and a cold, hard edge wrapped itself around his heart. The nebulous plan still forming in his mind was looking better and better by the moment.

"If you screw this up, you could be risking your son," Mick reminded him unnecessarily.

"No," Simon said, glancing back over his shoulder at his friend. "Don't you get it? A *Hawthorne* is in charge of whether or not I'm fit to care for my son. How could I possibly make that any worse?"

"Let me count the ways," Mick muttered darkly.

"You'll see," Simon told him, warming to his plan even as it took final shape in his mind. "I'm going to seduce Tula—" *again,* he added silently "—until she can't think straight. By the time I'm finished, she'll support me getting custody of Nathan. And when I'm sure of that, I'll go to her father and tell him that I've been sleeping with his daughter. If that doesn't give the old man a stroke, nothing will."

"What'll it do to her?" Mick asked quietly.

For one brief second, Simon considered that. Considered how it would be when she found out that she'd been used by him. But he let that thought go as soon as he remembered that she was a Hawthorne and that her family was more than accustomed to using and being used.

"Doesn't matter," he ground out.

"Whatever you say." Mick stood up and shook his head. "I'm heading home now, but before I go, one more piece of advice."

"I'm not going to like it, am I?"

Mick shrugged. "Whoever likes unsolicited advice?"

"Good point. Okay, let's have it."

"Don't do it."

"Do what?"

"Whatever it is you're planning, Simon." Mick locked his gaze with his friend's and said in all seriousness, "Just let this go."

Simon shook his head. "Hawthorne cheated me."

"His daughter didn't."

"She lied to me. About who she was. Maybe about why she's in my damn house."

"You don't know that. You could just ask her."

Sending a warning glare at his friend, Simon said, "You don't understand."

"You're right," Mick told him, turning for the door.

"I don't. For the last week or so, you've been almost… happy. I'd hate to see you screw that up for yourself, Simon."

He didn't say anything as Mick left. Hell, what was there to say? There was an opportunity here. A chance to get back at Jacob Hawthorne while at the same time indulging himself in a woman he wanted more than he was comfortable admitting.

An image of Tula filled his mind and his body went hard and heavy almost instantly. Remembering how responsive she was in bed had him wanting her so desperately, he'd have done anything to have her that minute. Even that damned fight they'd had hadn't cooled him off any. Instead, it had stoked the fires already inside him. He'd never enjoyed a fight more.

Didn't mean anything though, he told himself. Yes, he'd admitted to liking her. But that was before he knew who she really was. Now he didn't know if he could believe the person she'd shown herself to be. Maybe it was all an act. Maybe everything she had done since arriving at his house had all been part of an elaborate show.

If it was, he would have the last laugh. If it wasn't… he shook his head. He wouldn't consider that. Tula *Hawthorne* was a grown woman. She could make her own decisions. And if she decided to join him in his bed—and she would, *again*—that would be her choice.

She'd be fine.

He'd have his revenge.

And his son.

* * *

"He was a complete jerk," Tula said into her cell phone, then caught the baby watching her warily. She didn't care what some people thought about children and their awareness to the world around them. She knew that Nathan was sensitive to tone and her moods, so she instantly forced a smile, despite the sheen of ice that felt as though it was coating her insides.

"Honey," Anna's sympathetic voice came over the phone. "You're the one who always reminded me that most men are jerks at one point or another."

"Yes, but at *that* point?" Tula said in a hiss, still smiling for Nathan's sake. "Seriously, Anna the glow hadn't even begun to fade and he turned on me like a rabid dog."

"Well, I hope you gave it right back to him."

"I did," she said, remembering their fight last night. It had completely colored everything that went before it and that was saying something.

Sex with Simon had been even more amazing than she had imagined it could be. But to have it all ruined because Simon had donned his metaphorical suit right after was just infuriating.

"Nothing I said got through to him though, so it hardly matters that I fought back," she mused, plucking a windblown brown leaf from the blanket and tossing it into the air. "He was so cold. So…"

"Believe me I know," Anna assured her. "Remember how awful Sam was in the beginning?"

"That's different."

"Really, how?"

Tula laughed halfheartedly. "Because this is about *me*."

"Ah, well sure. Now I see."

Another laugh shot from Tula's throat helplessly. "Fine, fine. You suffered, all women suffer. But *my* suffering is happening now."

"Okay, there you've got me."

"Thanks. So. Advice?"

"Plenty, but advice isn't what you need, Tula. You already know how to handle this."

"Really, how's that?"

"Get Simon ready for Nathan and then come home. Where you belong."

Where she belonged.

For so many years, the tiny house in Crystal Bay had been just that. Tula's haven. The one spot in the world where she felt as if she'd carved out a place for herself. But now, thinking about going back to her old life of work and friends sounded somehow…empty.

Her gaze turned on the baby laying on a blanket spread over the grass of Simon's backyard. She didn't know if she *could* go back home. Her small house would now be crowded with memories of a baby that had brightened it so briefly. She would hear Nathan's cries in the night, find his toys tucked under the couch. She would wonder, always, how he was, what he was doing.

Just as she would wonder about Simon.

The bastard.

How dare he make her care for him and then become just…a *man?* How could he have experienced what they had shared and then turn his back on it all so mechanically? How could he simply flip a mental switch and shut off his emotions as easily as turning off a lightbulb?

Or maybe she was reading too much into him.

Giving him too much credit. Maybe he didn't *have* any emotions. Maybe that suit that so defined him had stunted any natural human feelings. Hadn't she warned herself the very first day she had met him that he was too much like her father? Too caught up in the world of corporate finances for her to be interested in him?

She should have listened to herself.

Then she remembered the look on his face as he had stared down at Nathan, knowing the baby was his son. His features had been easy enough to read. The man was capable of love. He simply wasn't interested in it.

At least, not with her.

"Yoo-hoo?"

"Huh? What?" Tula shook her head and said, "Sorry, sorry. Wasn't listening."

"Yeah, I got that," Anna said wryly. "You're not ready to come home yet, are you?"

"I can't. The baby and—"

"No." Anna's voice was soft and filled with understanding sympathy. "I mean, you're not ready to walk away from Simon yet, are you?"

Tula's shoulders slumped in resignation, though her friend couldn't see it. "No, guess I'm not. That makes me some kind of grand idiot, doesn't it?" Then, without waiting for her friend's response, she answered her own question. "Of course it does. Why would I think I could have feelings for a man so much like my father? Why didn't I stop myself?"

"Because sometimes you just can't, honey." Anna laughed. "Look at me! I took that mural job Sam offered me because I needed the money. I even told him to his face that I couldn't stand him! Now look where I am…

married and pregnant. Sometimes, the heart just wants what it wants and you can't do anything to change it."

"Well, that's not fair at all."

"And so little is," Anna commiserated. "Now, back to my original question with this phone call...do you still want me to come to the city this weekend? Do the mural on Nathan's wall?"

Tula thought about that. Knew Simon would probably hate it—he of the beige-with-cream-trim designing skills. Then Tula looked at the baby, waving his little arms at the naked tree branches high overhead. And she knew that if she couldn't be with him, then at least she could leave behind a physical reminder of her presence. One that both Nathan and Simon would see every day.

"Yeah, I do," Tula told her friend. "Nathan's room needs some brightening up."

"Great! I've already got some fabulous ideas."

"I trust you," Tula said, then added, "I've only got one request."

"What's that?"

"Paint in the Lonely Bunny somewhere, will you?" She reached out and smoothed her fingertips along Nathan's cheek. "That way it will almost be like I'm still here, watching over him. Even after I'm gone."

"Oh, sweetie..."

She heard the sympathy in her friend's voice and steeled herself against it. Tula didn't want pity. In fact, she wasn't sure what exactly she *did* want. Beyond Simon, of course, and that was never going to happen.

It would have been easier to seduce Tula if they hadn't already been to bed only to have the fight that had left both of them furious.

But Simon was nothing if not determined.

He dismissed Mick's warnings that seemed to repeat over and over again in his mind. After all, Mick was married. He and Katie had been together since college. They fit together so well, it was hard to believe they hadn't started out life joined at the hip. So how could his best friend understand the tension, the stubborn refusal to back down once a position was taken? How could he know anything about the sexual heat that flared during an argument?

How could he ever understand the enmity Simon felt for the Hawthorne family?

Simon knew exactly what he was doing—as he always did. And the fact that Mick disagreed wasn't going to stop him.

This plan of his was going to kill two birds with one impressive stone, he told himself. Not only would he be able to indulge himself with Tula—something he hadn't been able to stop thinking of—but he'd also have the revenge on her father that he had been dreaming of for three years. It would absolutely fry that old man when he found out that his daughter had been in Simon's bed.

But first things first. Before his plan could get into motion, Simon had to start making arrangements for when he had custody of Nathan. He wouldn't have Tula to care for the baby while he was at work, so he would need someone responsible for the job.

He didn't let himself think about the fact that when that day came, Tula would be out of their lives.

Nine

An hour later, he was home early again and didn't even stop to admit that since Tula had come into his life, he'd found less and less reason for hanging around the company. Instead, he seemed to be drawn to this old house and the woman inside it.

Simon found Tula in the backyard, watching Nathan squirm on a blanket beneath the winter sun. She turned to look at him and he could actually *see* her freeze up. A part of him regretted being the cause of that. He was too accustomed to her easy smile and ready laugh. Seeing her so wary, so cold, gave him a pause that none of Mick's not so subtle warnings had managed to do.

But he reminded himself that she was a Hawthorne and had never bothered to mention it. How much did he owe her anyway? Besides, he had a plan now and once Simon picked a direction, he didn't deviate. That would indicate that he doubted himself and he never did that.

Stuffing his hands into the pockets of his slacks, he walked down the flagstone steps that led to the landscaped yard. Each step was slow, deliberately careless, letting her know that though she might be angry, he was just fine.

Liar.

His brain shouted out that single word and he recognized the truth in it. But damned if he'd let her know.

"Isn't it a little cold out here for him?" Simon asked, nodding at the boy who was wearing a shoulder-to-toes zip-up blanket sleeper.

"Fresh air's good for him," she said stiffly. She countered, "You're home early."

He grinned, pleased that she'd noticed. "I am. I wanted to talk to you."

"Oh, can't wait," she said, sarcasm coloring her tone. "Our last conversation went so well."

Good, he told himself. She was still bothered. He liked knowing that what they'd shared had hit her as hard as it had him. And more, he wanted to share it all again. A lot.

He took a seat beside her on the blanket and hid a smile when she scooted away a bit. As if she didn't trust herself too near him. He knew just how she felt.

At the moment, all he really wanted to do was grab her and hold her and—

"What can you possibly have left to say that you didn't say last night?"

"Plenty," he admitted, drawing one knee up and resting his forearm on it.

"Let me guess," she said, her blue eyes snapping with banked fury. "You've found a way to blame me for global warming? Or am I a spy of some kind, sent to ferret out all of your secrets and feed them to your enemies?"

He just stared at her. Was that last statement for show or was she actually trying to tell him why she was really there? "Is that a confession?"

"Oh, for heaven's sake, Simon," she snapped in a whispered hiss. "You know darn well it's not. I'm just trying to guess how you'll insult me next."

He wondered, but let it go for now. "As a matter of fact, I don't want to talk about you at all," he said. "Now that we're committed to getting me ready to take over custody of Nathan, we have to find a competent nanny."

"A *nanny?*" she asked in the same tone she might have used to ask, *You want to hire an axe murderer?*

He nodded, pleased with her reaction. Even if he was confused about her motivation for being there, with him, he knew for a fact that she loved Nathan.

"I'll still have to work, so when you leave, I'll need someone here with the baby. I think a live-in nanny would be the best way to go, don't you?"

"I don't know," she said, glancing down at the babbling baby. "I hadn't really thought about someone else caring for him on a day-to-day basis."

Actually, Simon didn't much care for the idea of a stranger in his house taking care of his son while he wasn't there. But he couldn't see any way around it, either. No matter how his plan ended up working out, Tula wouldn't be here for him and Nathan to count on.

He really didn't like the thought of that, but refused to explore the reasons why.

"He can't go to work with me," Simon said abruptly, watching her reaction.

"No, I suppose not."

"Is there a problem?"

Her gaze flicked to his, fired for an instant, then cooled off again until those beautiful blue eyes of hers shone like the surface of a frozen lake. "No. No problem."

"Good," he said. "So I'll call the employment agency and have them send people over. Are you interested in interviewing them or would you prefer I do it?"

She looked torn and he was forced to admit silently that he felt the same way. Funny, this conversation about hiring a nanny didn't have anything to do with his plan. It had only seemed like a reasonable way for him to open communications with Tula again. Besides, theoretically, a caretaker for Nathan had sounded acceptable enough.

In practice though…looking down at his son—innocent, helpless, at the mercy of whoever his father hired to look after him…it felt wrong, somehow. Instantly, half-forgotten news reports flashed through his mind, stories about nannies and babysitters and preschools, all of whom were supposedly devoted caregivers. And how the children in their charge had paid the price for their negligence or apathy.

Frowning, Simon told himself this situation would be different. He would have the nanny he hired screened completely. He wouldn't trust just anyone with his son's safety.

But the scowl on his face deepened as he realized

that the only person he really trusted with Nathan's well-being was the woman beside him. The very woman who he already knew to be a liar. She hadn't told him the truth about who she was, so why should he trust her?

But he did. Instinctively, he knew he could trust Tula with his son. But she was also the woman who would be leaving someday soon.

The woman he was planning on using for his own taste of revenge.

Tula thanked the woman for coming and once she'd seen her out, closed the door and leaned back against it. A sigh of defeat slid from her throat.

That was the third prospective nanny she had interviewed in the last two days and she hadn't liked any of them.

"What was wrong with that one?"

Startled, she looked up at Simon, leaning against the newel post of the banister. His eyes were amused and his mouth was curved at one end as if he were trying to hide a smile that hadn't quite made it to his features.

"What're you doing here?" He had the most disconcerting habit of sneaking up on a person. And this new habit of his, splintering the routine he had clung to when she first came to the city, was even more disquieting. He was up to something, she figured. She just didn't know what. Which just put her that much more on guard.

He tossed his suit jacket over the newel post and loosened his red silk tie. "I live here, as I've pointed out before."

"Yes, but it's the middle of the afternoon. On a workday. Are you sick?"

He chuckled. "No, I'm not sick. I just left the office early. No big deal. Now, what was wrong with the woman you just sent packing?"

Still wary, she asked, "Didn't you see the bun she was wearing?"

"Bun?"

She saw the confusion on his face and explained. "Her hair. It was pulled into a taut little knot at the back of her head."

"So? An unattractive hairstyle makes for a bad nanny?"

It sounded silly when he said it, but Tula was going with her instincts. Nathan was too important to take any chances with his safety and happiness. She would find the *right* nanny for him or she just wouldn't leave.

Unless, she thought, that's exactly what she was subconsciously hoping for. That she could stay. That she could be the one raising Nathan, loving him. A worry for another day, she supposed.

"The woman's hair was scraped so tightly, her eyelids were tilted back. Anyone that rigid shouldn't be in charge of a child."

"Ah," he said as though he understood, but she knew he didn't. He was patronizing her.

"So the one yesterday afternoon, with her hair long and loose and curling...?"

She scowled at him. "Too careless. If she doesn't care what her hair looks like, she won't care enough about Nathan."

"And the first one?"

"She had mean eyes," Tula said with no apologies. She just knew that woman was the kind who made children sit in dark closets or go to bed without dinner. She would never leave Nathan with a cold-eyed woman.

Simon's eyebrow lifted again. She was getting to the point where she could judge his moods by the tilt of that eyebrow alone. Right now, she told herself with an inner grumble, he was entertained. By *her.*

Perhaps he had a point. Tula knew what she was doing wasn't fair to the women who had come looking for a job. Except for the mean-eyed one, they seemed nice enough. Certainly qualified. The agency Simon was dealing with was the top one in the city, known for representing the absolute best in nannies.

But how could she be expected to turn over a little boy she loved to a stranger?

He was still watching her with just the barest hint of amusement on his face. An expression she found way too attractive for her own well-being.

"All right," she conceded grudgingly, "maybe I'm being a little too careful in the selection process."

"Maybe?"

She ignored that. Because even if she was being overprotective, it wouldn't hurt that baby any. It would only help ensure that the best possible person would be in charge of him. And if anything, as the baby's father, Simon should appreciate that.

"This is important, Simon. No one knows better than I do just how much the people in a child's life can impact their character. The way they look at the world. The way they think of themselves."

She caught herself when she realized that she was headed in a verbal direction she had had no intention of going.

"Speaking from experience," he mused and she knew

he was remembering the story she'd told him about the bunny she had once tried to befriend. And about her mother's less than maternal attitude toward her.

"Is that so surprising?" she countered. "Doesn't everyone have some sort of issue with their parents? Even the best of them make mistakes, right?"

"True," he acknowledged, but his gaze never left hers. She felt as if he were trying to see inside her mind. To read her thoughts and display all of her secrets.

As if to prove her right, he spoke again.

"Who had that impact on you, Tula?" he asked, voice quiet. "Was it just your mom?"

"This isn't about me," she told him, refusing to be drawn into the very discussion she had unwittingly initiated.

"Isn't it?" he asked, pushing away from the banister to walk toward her.

"No," she insisted with a shake of her head. She felt the intensity of his gaze and flinched from it. Tula didn't need sympathy and wasn't interested in sharing her childhood miseries with a man who had already made it clear just how he felt about her. "This is about Nathan and what's best for him."

He kept coming and was close enough now that she had to hold her breath to keep from inhaling the scent of him. A blend of his aftershave and soap, it was a scent that called to her, made her remember lying beneath him, staring up into his eyes as they flashed with passion. Eyes that were, at the moment, studying her.

"You said it yourself," he told her, "we're all affected by who raised us. And whoever raised you will affect who you choose to care for Nathan."

Instantly, her back went up. He'd somehow touched on the one thing that had given her a lot of misgivings over the years. She had thought about how she was raised and about her parents and had wondered if she should even have a child of her own. But the truth was, Tula's heart yearned for family. Hungered for the kind of love and warmth she used to dream about. And she had always known she would be a good parent because she knew just what a child wanted. Craved.

So she was completely prepared and ready to argue this point with Simon.

"No, Simon. You're wrong about that. The initial input a child is given is important, I agree. And when we're kids and growing up, it pushes us in one direction or another. But at some point, responsible adults make choices. *We* decide who we are. Who we want to be."

He frowned as he thought about what she said. "Do we? I wonder. Seems to me that we are always who we started out to be."

Uncomfortable with being so close to him and unable to touch, she walked into the living room. She wished Nathan were awake right now because then she could claim that she didn't have time to talk. That she had to take care of the baby. But it was nap time and that baby really enjoyed his naps. Ordinarily, she loved that about him because she could get a lot of her own work done. Today, when she could have used Nathan's presence, she had to admit there would be no help coming from that quarter.

She kept walking farther into the huge room and didn't stop until she was standing in front of the bay window. Naturally, Simon followed her, his footsteps sure and slow, sounding out easily against the wood floor.

"So," he said, "you're saying your parents had nothing to do with who you are today?"

Tula laughed to herself but kept the sound quiet, so he wouldn't know just how funny that statement really was. Of course her parents had shaped her. Her mom was a lovely woman who was simply never meant to be a mother. Katherine was more at home with champagne brunches than PTA meetings. Impatient with clumsiness or loud noises, Katherine preferred a more formal atmosphere—one without the clamor of children.

Being responsible for a child had cut into Katherine's lifestyle, though it had significantly increased her alimony when she and Jacob divorced.

But when her stint at motherhood was complete, Katherine left. She moved out of Crystal Bay the morning of her daughter's eighteenth birthday.

Tula still remembered that last hug and brief conversation.

The airport was crowded, of course, with people coming and going. Excitement simmered in the air alongside sorrow as lovers kissed goodbye and family members waved and promised to write.

"You'll be fine, Tula," her mother said as she moved toward her gate. "You're all grown up now, I've done my job and you're entirely capable of taking care of yourself."

Tula wanted to ask her mother to stay. She wanted to tell Katherine that she so wasn't ready to be alone. That she was a little scared about college and the future. But it would have been pointless and she knew that, too. A part of her mother was already gone. Her mind and heart were fixed in Italy, just waiting for her body to catch up.

Katherine was renting a villa outside Florence for the summer, then she would be moving on—to where, Tula had no idea. The only thing she was absolutely sure of was that her mother wouldn't be back.

"Now, I can't miss boarding, so give me a kiss."

Tula did, and fought the urge to hug her mom and hold on. Sure, her mother had never been very maternal, but she had been there. Every day. In the house that would now be empty. That would echo with her own thoughts rattling around in the suffocating silence.

Her father was in the city and Tula wouldn't be seeing him anytime soon, so she was truly on her own for the first time ever. And though she could admit to a certain amount of anticipation, the inherent scariness of the situation was enough to swamp everything else.

Thank God, Tula thought, she still had Anna Cameron and her family. They would be there for her when she needed them. They always had been. That knowledge made saying goodbye to her mother a bit easier, though no less sad.

She'd often dreamed that she and her mother could be closer. She had wished she had the sense of family that Anna had. Though Anna's mom had died when she was a girl, her father and stepmother had supported and loved her. But wishes changed nothing, she told herself firmly, then pasted a bright smile on her face.

"Enjoy Italy, Mom. I'll be fine."

"I know you will, Tula. You're a good girl."

Then she was gone, not even bothering to glance back to see if her daughter was still watching.

Which Tula was.

She stood alone and watched until the plane pulled away from the gate. Until it taxied to the runway. Until it took off and became nothing more than a sun-splashed dot in the sky.

Finally, Tula went home to an empty house and promised herself that one day she would build a family. She would have what she had always longed for.

Simon was watching her, waiting for her to answer his question. She scrubbed her hands up and down her arms and said, "Of course they influenced me. But not in the way you might think. I didn't want to be who they were. I didn't want what they wanted. I made a conscious decision to be myself. *Me*. Not just a twig on the family tree."

A flash of surprise lit his eyes and she wondered why.

"How's that working out for you?"

"Until today," she admitted, "pretty good."

He walked closer and Tula backed up. She was feeling a little vulnerable at the moment and the last thing she needed was to be too near Simon. She kept moving until the backs of her knees hit the ledge of the cushioned window seat. Abruptly, she sat down and her surprise must have shown on her face.

He chuckled and asked, "Am I making you nervous, Tula?"

"Of course not," she replied, while her mind was screaming, *Yes!* Everything about him was suddenly making her nervous and she wasn't sure how to handle it. Since she'd met him, he'd irritated her, intrigued her. But this anxiousness was a new sensation.

Tula knew everyone thought of her as flaky. The crazy artist. But she wasn't really. She had always known what she wanted. She lived the way she liked and made no apologies for it. She always knew who was in her life and what they meant to her.

At least, she had until Simon. But he was a whole different ball game. He went from insulting her to seducing her. He made her furious one moment and hot and achy the next. For a man who had so loved his routine, he was becoming entirely too unpredictable.

She couldn't seem to pin him down. Or guess what he was going to do or say. She had thought him just another staid businessman, but he was more than that. She simply wasn't sure what that meant for her. Which made her a little nervous, though she'd never admit to it. So to keep herself steady, she started talking again.

"You've heard my story, so tell me, how did wearing a three-piece suit by the age of two affect you?"

He gave her a half smile and sat down beside her on the window seat. Turning his head, he stared through the glass at the winter afternoon behind them.

A storm was piling up on the horizon, Tula saw as she followed his gaze. Thunderclouds huddled together in a dark gray mass that promised rain by evening. Already, the wind was picking up, sending the naked branches of the trees in the park into a frenzied dance. Mothers gathered up their children as the sky darkened further and soon the park was as empty as Tula felt.

When Simon finally spoke, his voice was so soft, she nearly missed it. "You think you've got me figured out, do you?"

She studied him, trying to read his eyes. But it was as if he'd drawn a shutter over them, locking himself away from her.

"I thought so," she admitted and her confusion must

have been evident in her tone. "When I first met you, you reminded me of…someone I used to know," she said, picturing her father, fierce gaze locked on some hapless employee. "But the more I got to know you, the more I realized that I didn't know you at all. Well, that made no sense," she ended with a laugh.

"Yeah, it did," Simon said, shifting to look at her again, closing off the outside world with the intensity of his gaze. Making her feel as if she were the only thing in the world that mattered at the moment.

"Simon…"

"Nobody is what they look like on the surface," he murmured, features carefully blank and unreadable as he studied her. "I'm just really realizing that."

Ten

He was looking at her as if he had never seen her before. As if he were trying to see into her heart and mind again, searching out her secrets. Her desires.

"I don't know what you mean," Tula said.

"Maybe I don't, either." He took a breath, blew it out and after a long, thoughtful moment, changed the subject abruptly. "You know, I grew up here, in this house. My great-grandfather built it originally."

"It's a lovely house," she said, briefly allowing her gaze to sweep the confines of the room. "It feels *warm*."

"Yeah, it does." His gaze was still locked on her. "Now, more than ever."

Why was he telling her this? Why was he being… nice? Weren't they at odds? Didn't their argument still hang in the air between them? Only a few minutes ago, he had looked at her with cool detachment and now everything felt different. She just didn't understand *why*.

"Several years ago, my father almost lost the house," he said, forcing an offhand attitude that didn't mesh with the sudden stiffness of his shoulders or the tightness in his jaw. "Bad investments, trusting the wrong people. My dad didn't have a head for business."

"I can sympathize," she muttered, remembering how many times her own father had made her feel small and ignorant because she hadn't cared to learn the intricacies of keeping ledgers and accounts receivable.

He kept talking, as if she hadn't spoken at all. "He was too unorganized. Couldn't keep anything straight." Shaking his head, he once more stared out at the gathering storm and focused on the windowpane as the first drops of rain plopped against it. But Tula knew he wasn't looking at the outside world so much as he was staring into his own past. Just as she had moments ago.

"My dad entered a deal once with a man who was so unscrupulous he damn near succeeded in taking this house out from under us. This man cheated and lied and did whatever he had to in his effort to bury my father and the Bradley family in general." Simon shook his head again. "My father never saw it coming, either. It was sheer luck that kept this house in the family. Luck that saved what was left of our business."

She heard the old anger in his voice and wondered who it was that had almost cost his family so much. Whoever it was, Simon was still furious with the man and she wished she could say something that would ease that feeling. Tula knew all too well that hanging on to anger didn't hurt the one it was focused on. It only made *you* miserable.

"I'm glad it worked out that way," she said simply. "I can't imagine how hard it must have been for your father. And you."

He looked at her as if judging what she'd said, trying to decide if she had meant it. Finally though, he accepted her words with a nod. "In a way, I guess it wasn't my dad's fault. He went into the family business because his father wanted it that way. My dad hated his life, knew he wasn't any good at it and that must have been hard, living with a sense of failure every day."

"I know what that's like."

He tipped his head to one side and narrowed his eyes. "Do you?"

She smiled, actually enjoying this quiet time with him. The talking, the sharing of old pains and secrets. She had never really talked about her father with anyone but Anna. But somehow, it seemed right now, to let Simon know that he wasn't alone in his feelings about the past.

"My father had plans for me, too," she said sadly. "And they didn't have anything to do with what I wanted."

He nodded again thoughtfully. "For me, I watched what happened with my dad and I learned."

"What?" she prompted, her voice soft and low. "You learned what?"

His eyes narrowed as he watched her and Tula felt the heat of his stare slide into her bones.

"I learned to pay attention. To make rules and follow them. To never let anyone get the best of me. There's no room in my life for chaos, Tula," he said.

There was no subtext there and she knew it. He was saying flat out that there was no room in his life for *her.* She had figured that out for herself, of course. But somehow hearing him say it out loud left a hollow feeling in the pit of her stomach.

"I saw exactly what happens when a man loses focus," Simon added. "My dad couldn't concentrate on work he hated, so he didn't pay attention. I never lose focus. I guess I did the same thing you did. Made my own choices in spite of the early training by my father."

And those choices would keep them apart. He couldn't have been any clearer. So why, she wondered, was he looking at her as if he wanted nothing more than to grab her and carry her up to his bed? Heat filled his eyes even as a chill colored his words. The man was a walking contradiction and Tula really wished she didn't find that so darned attractive.

She shook her head as if to rid herself of that thought and asked, "What about your mother? Didn't she have some impact on you, too?"

"No," he said abruptly. "She died in a car wreck when I was four. Don't remember her at all."

"'I'm sorry' doesn't sound like much," she told him, "but I am."

"Thanks." He looked at her again and this time there was emotion glittering in his eyes. She just wished she could decipher it. Simon Bradley touched her in ways she had never experienced before. Even knowing that nothing was going to come of what was simmering between them couldn't stop her from wishing things were different.

Wishing that just once in her life, someone would see her for who she was and want her.

"Tell me more about your father," Simon said suddenly. "What's he like?"

"Like you," she blurted without thinking.

"Excuse me?"

Tula thought it a little weird that he could look so insulted without even knowing who her father was. "What I mean is, he's a businessman, too. He practically lives in his office and can't see anything in his life if it's not on his profit-loss statements. He's a workaholic and he likes it that way."

He leaned back against a pillow tucked up to the wall. "And that's how you see me?"

"Well, yeah." Grateful to be off the subject of her own family, Tula said, "You're a lot like him. Go to work early, come home late—"

"I'm home early today. Have been for the last few days."

"True and I don't know what to make of that."

"I intrigue you?"

"You confuse me."

"Even better."

"No," she said, inching back on the window seat to keep plenty of room between them. "It's really not, Simon. I don't need more confusion in my life and you've already made it pretty clear what you think about me."

"That fight we had, you mean?"

"Yes."

"Didn't mean a thing," he told her and leaned forward.

"That's not how you felt *then*," she reminded him, trying not to notice that he was just within reach of her.

"As I remember it, you had plenty to say, too."

"Okay, yes. I did. You made me mad."

"Oh, trust me, you made that perfectly clear."

"Good then. We both remember that argument."

"That's not all we remember," he said, voice low, thick. He reached for her hand before she could pull back and rubbed his thumb across her palm.

Tula shivered. It wasn't her fault, she thought frantically. It's not like she *chose* to be this attracted to him. It was simple chemistry. A biological imperative. Simon touched her and she went up in flames.

But she could choose to step back from the fire.

"Simon..."

"Tula, we were good together."

"In bed, sure, but—"

"Let's just concentrate on the bed for right now, huh?"

Oh, that sounded really good, she silently admitted. That featherlight touch on her palm was already firing up every nerve ending in her body. She took a breath, held it, then released it on a sigh.

Oh, Tula, she thought wildly, *you're going to do it, aren't you?*

Even as that disappointed-in-herself sigh wound through her mind, Tula was leaning in toward Simon.

It was inevitable.

Her gaze locked with his as his mouth touched hers. A whispered groan slid from her throat at that first, gentle contact. And she realized just how much she'd missed him. Missed *this*. It didn't seem to matter that they were constantly butting heads. He was right. For now, all she had to concentrate on was what she felt when she was with him. When she surrendered herself to the magic of his touch, his kiss.

No doubt, there would be plenty of time for regrets in the coming weeks and months. For right now there was only *him*.

As if a floodgate had been opened somewhere inside her, emotions churned, fast and furious throughout her system. She leaned in closer, allowing him to deepen the kiss. His arms closed around her, holding her tightly to his chest and suddenly, the wide window seat seemed too narrow. Too public.

He tumbled her to the floor, assuring that he landed on the hardwood and she was cushioned against his chest.

Her breath left her in a whoosh of sound. She lifted her head, looked down into his eyes and grinned. "You okay?"

He winced, then smiled back. "I'm fine. And I'm about to be better."

"Promises, promises…"

A wide smile dazzled his eyes and made her heartbeat jump into a gallop. His hands swept up and down her spine and paused long enough to give her behind a quick squeeze.

"I know a challenge when I hear one," he said and lifted his head from the floor to kiss her again. Harder, deeper, his tongue swept past her defenses and tangled with hers in a sensual dance that stole her breath.

She cupped his face in her palms, loving the feel of his whiskers against her skin. She shivered as his arms tightened around her, holding her so closely she could feel the pounding of his heartbeat shuddering through her.

He rolled over, cradling her in his arms until she was on her back and his heavy weight pressed down on her. Tula sighed, loving the feel of him on top of her. She didn't mind the hardness of the floor beneath her, because he was too busy making sure she felt nothing but pleasure.

He tore his mouth from hers, buried his face in the curve of her neck and nibbled at her throat, sending tiny jolts of sensation across her skin. Tula fought for breath and ran her hands up and down his broad back. His heavy muscles tensed and flexed beneath her fingertips and she smiled at the knowledge of how much her touch affected him.

Staring up at the beamed ceiling overhead, Tula lost herself in the flash of heat swamping her. His hands moved over her body with finesse and determination. He left trails of fire in his wake. She felt as though she were burning up from the inside and all she could think of was the need for even more flames.

His mouth moved over her skin, her throat, her jaw and up again to her mouth where he kissed her until she couldn't breathe, couldn't think. Only sensation was left to her.

Then passion crashed down on them both in the same searing instant. Hands moved quickly, freeing buttons, undoing snaps and zippers and in seconds, they were naked, entwined tightly together on the living room floor.

Rain beat a counterpoint to the gasps and moans sounding out in the dimly lit room. From outside came the muffled heartbeat of the world. Cars whizzing past, wheels on wet streets sounding like steaks sizzling on a grill. Wind rattled the windowpanes and sighed beneath the eaves. From the nearby monitor came the quiet, steady breathing of the child upstairs in his bed.

And none of those sounds were enough to intrude on this moment. Around them, the world continued. But in that room, time stood still. There was only the two of them, Tula thought. Just she and Simon and for this one amazing instant she was going to forget about everything else. Stop trying to read the future, or hide from the past, long enough to enjoy the present.

Instead, she would lose herself in a pair of chocolate-brown eyes that saw too much and revealed too little.

"You're thinking," he accused, one corner of his mouth lifting into a half smile.

"Sorry," she said, smoothing her fingertips across his jaw. "Don't know how that happened."

"Let's just see what I can do about shutting down that busy brain of yours."

"Think you're up to the challenge?" she teased.

"Baby," he assured her, "I'm *very* up for it."

A surprised laugh shot from her throat and Tula sighed with happiness. Having a lover who could make her laugh at the most astonishing times, was really a gift. And maybe, she thought, there were even *more* layers to Simon Bradley than she had assumed. Maybe—

Then he began his quest to shut off her thoughts and he was more than successful. Tula groaned when his mouth came down on her breast. He licked and nibbled and she twisted beneath him, trying to take more of what he offered. Needing to feel all she could of him. Needing—just *needing.*

He suckled her and she gasped, arching into him, holding his head to her breast, as his mouth pulled at her breast. Her fingers speared through his thick, soft hair. She loved the feel of his mouth on her and thought frantically that she could happily spend the rest of her life like this.

He smiled against her skin. She felt the curve of his mouth against her breast and she knew he was aware of the effect he had on her. But she wasn't interested in hiding it from him anyway. Why shouldn't he know that he could splinter her body and shatter her soul with a kiss? A touch?

The wood floor beneath her bare back was cool, but the heat he built within her was more than a match for it. He lay between her thighs and she felt the tip of him prodding at her center. She wanted that invasion of body into body. Wanted to feel the slick slide of his heat into hers.

She lifted her hips in silent welcome, but he didn't respond to her invitation. Instead, he rolled over, taking her with him until she was splayed atop him, staring down into those eyes that fascinated her so.

"The floor's not real comfortable," he told her, reaching up to cup her breasts in the palms of his hands. "Thought we'd just change position for awhile."

"Change is good," she said, straddling him, keeping her gaze fixed on his. Her hands moved over his sculpted chest. At her touch, he hissed in a breath.

Simon looked up at her and felt his mind blur. He'd been planning this seduction for days and now that it was here, his plans meant nothing. The only thing that mattered was her. The feel of her. The taste of her. The soft sighs that drifted from her throat at his touch.

Shadowy light played on her choppy blond hair and winked off the silver hoops in her ears. Her big blue eyes were glazed with the same passion claiming him.

He kneaded her breasts with a firm, gentle touch and tweaked her hardened nipples between his thumbs and forefingers. He loved watching the play of emotion on her face as she hid nothing from him.

Her eager response to lovemaking only fed the fires inside him, pushing at him to take more, to give more. Her hips were rocking instinctively and his own body was hard and tight.

He set his hands at her hips and lifted her high enough off him that he could position himself to slide inside her. She closed her eyes, tipped her head back and, taking control of the situation, slowly, inch by inch, took him inside. She settled herself over him with a deliberately slow slide that was both tantalizing and exasperating. He tried to hurry her, to push himself into her harder, deeper, but the tiny, curvy woman was in control now, whether he liked it or not.

"You're just going to have to lay there and take it," she said, a sly, purely female smile on her lips.

His eyes crossed as she finally settled on top of him, with his body sheathed completely inside hers. She was tight and damp and so damn hot he couldn't think of anything but the sensations crashing down on him.

She moved, just a slight wiggle of her hips, but that small action shot through him with the force of a nine-point earthquake. He felt the world tremble. Or at least his corner of it. And he wanted more.

Didn't matter *why* he'd seduced her, he assured himself. All that mattered now was what they created together. The impossible heat. The incredible friction of two bodies moving as one toward a climax that would be, he knew, richer and more all-encompassing than anything else he'd ever known.

He didn't care who Tula was. Didn't want to remember that he was, in effect, setting her up to be used as a weapon against her own father. What he wanted to concentrate on now was how well they meshed. How their bodies joined so easily it was as if they were two pieces in the same puzzle.

She moved on him again, her hips rocking, taking him in and releasing him in a slow rhythm that built steadily into a pace that stole his breath and the last of his thoughts.

She arched her back, pushing her breasts higher. Her hands were on his chest, bracing herself as she rode him with a frenzied, honest passion that shook him to the core. Hands at her hips, he stared up into her eyes as she moved, and he was caught by the light glittering in those blue depths.

He felt swept up by both passion and emotion and just for that one, staggering moment, Simon forgot about everything else but Tula. She cried out his name as her release claimed her and a single heartbeat later, his body joined hers.

Blindly, Simon reached for her, pulling her down to his chest where he could cradle her close. Where, for a few brief seconds, he could forget that he had maneuvered her into this and instead pretend that what they had just shared was real.

Eleven

It had changed nothing.

And everything.

Two days later, Tula was still trying to understand the shift in her and Simon's relationship. If she could even call it that. Connected by a child, they were two people currently sharing a bed. Did that actually constitute a "relationship"?

Simon was kind and funny and warm and so attentive in bed, she'd hardly had any sleep at all the last two nights. Which, of course, she wasn't exactly complaining about. But was there anything else in his heart for her? Was it just desire? Was it expediency, since she was right there in his house and would be until she decided to hand over custody of Nathan?

She'd given herself to the man she loved with no assurances at all that he would care for her in return. Yes, she loved him. And it was too late now to change that.

How could she have let this happen? Hadn't she made a vow to herself not to take that last slippery step into love? But how could she possibly have avoided it? she asked herself. Simon was so much more than she had originally thought him to be. She had seen glimpses of his caring nature that he fought to bury so deeply. She had watched him with his son and been touched by the gentleness he showed Nathan. She had laughed with Simon, fought with him and made love with him in every possible way.

She couldn't avoid the simple truth any longer. She was in love with a man who was only in lust.

"This can't end well."

"That's the spirit," Anna cheered sarcastically.

Tula just looked at her friend and shook her head. "How you can expect me to be optimistic about this is beyond me. Anna, he doesn't love me."

"You don't know that."

A snort of laughter shot from her throat. "He hasn't said it. Hasn't shown any signs of admitting it. I think that's a good clue."

"All that means is that he's a man," Anna said, her gaze locked on the mural she was painting. "Sweetie, none of them ever want to admit to being in love. For some bizarre reason, the male brain deliberately will jump in the opposite direction the first time the word 'love' is used. They're just naturally skittish."

Tula laughed out loud. The baby on her hip enjoyed the sound and gurgled happily. She planted a quick kiss on his forehead before answering her friend.

"Simon? Skittish?" Shaking her head, she imagined the man in her mind and the idea of him being nervous about anything seemed even more ludicrous. "He's a force of nature, Anna. He sets down rules and expects everyone else to abide by them. And they *do*."

"You don't," she pointed out.

"No, but I'm different."

"He doesn't even expect you to do what he says, does he?"

"Not anymore," Tula assured her. "He knows better."

"Uh-huh." Anna maneuvered her paintbrush across the wall and still kept the conversation going. "So he's broken his own rule when it comes to you."

She thought about that for a second. "I suppose, but only because I made fun of his stupid schedule."

"How did he react?"

"He was all insulted," Tula told her with a laugh. Then she remembered. "But he started changing up his schedule. Coming home early, skipping meetings..."

"Hmm," Anna mused.

"That doesn't mean anything," Tula protested, but her mind was working.

"Only that Mr. I-have-a-schedule-set-in-stone is changing himself because of you."

"But—"

"Men don't do that if they don't care, Tula. Why would they?"

"No," Tula said, shaking her head, "you're wrong. Simon doesn't care about me. Beyond the obvious pluses about having me in his bed and here, taking care of Nathan."

"I don't know..."

"I do," Tula insisted, closing her mind to thoughts of Simon for a minute as she stared at the baby settled at her hip. She wasn't going to pretend everything was great. It wasn't. And it wasn't only the question of Simon's feelings that had her wrapped up so tightly.

Every day that passed she was that much closer to having to say goodbye to Nathan. She was going to lose the child that felt like her own. She was going to lose his father and the illusion of family she'd been living in for weeks. She was going to lose everything that mattered to her and that knowledge was tearing a hole in her heart.

"I'm going to have to leave soon, Anna. I'll have to walk away from Nathan *and* Simon. And the thought of it is just killing me."

Sitting back on her heels, Anna looked up at her. "Who are you and what have you done with Tula?"

"What's that supposed to mean?"

"It means that you are the world's biggest optimist," Anna told her, turning back to the mural she had been working on since the day before. "Even when you had no reason for it, you always maintained the upbeat attitude. Heck, Tula. Even your dad didn't rock your boat. If you wanted something, you went after it, no matter how many people tried to tell you it couldn't be done. So what's happening?"

Tula sat down, balancing Nathan in the circle of her crossed legs. "He did," she said, dropping a kiss onto the baby's head. "This little guy changed everything for me, Anna. I can't just go my own way anymore. Not when I have him to think about."

"Ah," her friend said, "so this isn't about Simon at all? You've been kidding yourself and me? You're just worried about Nathan, huh? Not pining away for the baby's father?"

Eyes narrowed, Tula warned, "No one likes a know-it-all."

"Oooh. Scored a point!" Smiling, Anna swept paint over the forest on the wall, wielding her paintbrush as expertly as a surgeon used his scalpel. "Come on, honey. This sudden case of the poor me's is about more than Nathan. More even than Simon. This is about you finally finding the place you want to be and thinking you have to leave it."

Tula cringed inside because Anna was exactly right.

"You found the home you've been looking for since you were a kid, sweetie." Anna looked at her, understanding and sympathy shining in her eyes. "You love Simon and Nathan both. But it's what they are to you together that's making this so hard. They're the family you always dreamed about. Your heart took them both in, made them yours and now you believe you have to let the dream die."

Nathan babbled and slapped playfully at Tula's hands on his legs. The scent of paint hung in the air despite the two opened windows. Anna's mural was almost complete. Once the woman got started on a painting, she was a whirlwind of activity. Tula looked at the realistic scene of a forest, with a flower-strewn meadow stretching out into the distance. And she smiled at Lonely Bunny, right up front, sitting under a tree and smiling out at the room.

From the house next door, the sound of wind chimes played like a distant symphony. As time passed in a lazy, unhurried way, Tula thought about what her friend had said and admitted silently that Anna was right. She did love Simon and Nathan both. She did love the family the three of them had become, however temporarily. She hated knowing that she was the one who didn't fit. The one who didn't belong. And knowing that she would have to walk away from what might have been was desolating.

"You're right," she finally said.

"The one time I wish I weren't," Anna told her.

"But what can I do? I can't stall Simon forever. He has a right to be his son's father. And I can't stay once I sign over custody."

"It's a problem," Anna agreed. "But there's always a solution. Somewhere."

Tula sighed. "You know, it was a lot easier on me when *you* were the one with man problems."

"I bet," Anna said on a laugh. "But it's your turn now, girl. The question is, what are you going to do about it?"

"What can I do?"

The last few days had been wonderful. And confusing. She had Nathan to care for and work of her own to accomplish during the day. But every night, she and Simon found each other. They shared taking care of Nathan, and once the baby was in bed it was their time.

The sex was incredible. It only got better each time they came together. But for Tula, it was bittersweet. She loved being with him—the problem was, she *loved* him. More than she had ever thought it possible to love someone. Every day here dragged her deeper and deeper into what was going to become a pit of despair one day soon.

Though even as she thought it, she realized that neither of them had so much as hinted about that situation lately.

It might still be the eight-hundred-pound gorilla in the middle of the room, but if no one was talking about it, did it matter?

Nathan babbled happily and Tula sighed.

"Honey, if you want him, why don't you go for it?"

"Oh, I am," she assured her friend.

Laughing, Anna said, "I'm not talking about sex, Tula. I'm talking about love. I know you love Simon. Heck, I can see it. Chances are he can, too."

"Oh, God," she said with a groan. "I hope not."

"Why?" Anna turned to look at her. "Why should you hide what you feel? Didn't you tell me to go for what I wanted?"

"Yes, but—"

"If he doesn't love you back, that's different." She rubbed her nose and transferred a streak of green paint. "Although, I'm willing to bet he does love you. I mean, how could he not? What's not to love? Besides, I saw you two together yesterday and again this morning. The way he looks at you..."

"What?" Hope rose up in Tula's chest.

"As if you're the only thing in the room," Anna said with a smile. "But Tula, you'll never know for sure what he feels if you don't try to get him to admit it."

"How am I supposed to do that?"

Anna grinned. "The best opportunity for getting a man to talk and lower his defenses at the same time? Right after sex. They're happy, they're relaxed and *very* open to suggestion."

Sometimes, she thought. Other times, they were too crabby entirely. Still it was worth a shot. Tula shook her head in admiration. "Does Sam know how truly devious you can be?"

"Sure he does," Anna replied, still grinning devilishly. "But by the time he figures out that I'm sneaking up on him, it's too late."

"I don't know..."

"Who was it who said all's fair in love and war?"

"I don't know that, either," Tula admitted. "But I'll bet it was a man."

"So," Anna said softly, "if it's okay for a man to be sneaky, why can't we try it? Look," she added, "while you're here, don't hold anything back. You can't tell him you love him, but you can show him. Make him want what you could have together. That's all I'm saying."

While her friend turned her attention back to the mural, and Nathan studied his toes with fierce concentration, Tula started thinking.

"You're going to do it, aren't you?"

"Do what?" Simon didn't take his gaze off the pitching machine. Getting hit by a ninety-mile-an-hour fastball didn't sound like a good time.

"Tula. You're going to mess it all up and toss it aside, aren't you?"

Simon hit the pitch high and left. Only then did he glance at Mick in the next cage over. "I don't know what you're talking about."

"Oh, forget it, Simon. I've known you too long to be fooled."

"Have you known me long enough to butt out?"

"Apparently not," Mick said good-naturedly. "Besides, you can always fire me if you don't like what I'm saying."

Simon snorted. "Sure. I fire you, then your wife comes over to kick my butt."

"There is that," Mick said, a pleased note in his voice. "So. About Tula."

"Let it go, Mick. I'm doing what I have to do."

"No," his friend insisted, "you're doing what your damn pride is telling you to do. There's a difference."

Simon hit a curveball dead center, line drive. "This isn't about my pride," he muttered darkly, irritated that his best friend wasn't on his side in this.

Mick was normally an excellent barometer for Simon. If the two of them agreed on something, it turned out to be a good idea. The times when Simon hadn't listened to Mick's advice were a different story. But this time, Mick was wrong. Simon knew it. He felt it.

Ever since her friend left last weekend, after painting a mural of a forest glade, complete with Lonely Bunny sitting beneath a tree, things had been...different.

Actually, the last few days with Tula had been great. Better than great. Amazing even. But it wasn't real. It had all been staged by him. They'd laughed and talked and gone for picnics and out to dinner. They took Nathan for walks and set him in a swing for the first time, making them both nervous. He had felt closer to her than he had to anyone else in his life, he thought darkly.

But none of Tula's responses to him were real because he had seduced her back into his bed for a deliberate reason. So if what he had done wasn't on the up-and-up, how could her reactions be genuine?

If he felt the occasional twinge of guilt over tricking her into being a weapon to use against her father...Simon dismissed the feeling. He didn't do guilt. Plus there was the fact that Tula was an adult, he assured himself, able to make her own choices. And she had *chosen* to be in his bed.

Yet, even as he told himself that, a voice in the back of his mind whispered the question, *Would she still have chosen to be with you if she knew what you were really doing? If she knew she was nothing more to you than a sword to wield against her father?*

Uncomfortable with what the answer to that might have been, he dismissed the mental question. Besides, he argued with himself, Tula wasn't *only* a weapon he'd waited years to find against Jacob Hawthorne. She was more, damn it. He actually…cared about her. Hadn't meant to, but he did.

Which was why he was standing at the batting cages arguing with himself while his best friend ragged on him. But the bottom line was, just because what he and Tula had together was mutually enjoyable, it didn't mean it was necessarily more than that, did it?

Besides, this wasn't even about Tula.

It was about her father.

After hearing what little she'd told him about her parents, she might even be grateful that he had found a way to take a slap at Jacob Hawthorne.

He snorted to himself and hit the next pitch, a slider, into right field. Sure. She'd *thank* him for using her. God, what universe was he living in anyway?

"This is all about your pride, Simon. You got cheated by a guy with no principles."

"Damn right I did," he snapped, turning his head to glare briefly at Mick. "And it wasn't just me, remember. Jacob maneuvered my father, too. That miserable old thief almost cost us our house, damn it."

He hated knowing that Jacob Hawthorne was out there, still chortling over getting the best of two generations of Bradleys. The need for revenge had been gnawing on him for years. Was he expected to now just put it aside because he had feelings for a woman? *Could* he put it aside?

"And your answer to that is to become as unprincipled as the old pirate himself?"

"What the hell are you talking about?"

Mick shook his head, clearly disgusted. "If you do this. If you use Tula to get at her old man, then you're as big a louse as he is."

Simon chewed on those words for a minute or two, then shook them off, determined to stay his course. He'd made a plan, damn it. Now he had to follow through. That was how he lived his life and he wasn't about to change now. Wasn't even sure he could change if he wanted to.

"It's not who you are, Simon," Mick told him. "I hope you remember that before it's too late."

A few days later, Tula was happy.

Anna had been right, she thought. Though she hadn't actually confessed her love for Simon, she had tried to show him over the last several days just how important he had become to her. She was sure she was getting through to him. She felt it. In his easy smile. His touch. The whispered words in the night and the gentle strength in his arms when he held her as she slept.

He hadn't mentioned again the subject of hiring a nanny. They hadn't talked about him taking full custody of Nathan. Instead, the three of them were in a sort of limbo. Locked into a paralyzing state where they didn't move forward and didn't go back. It was as if they were caught in the present, while Tula and Simon tried to decide what might be waiting for them in the still hazy future.

She didn't like waiting. She never had been a patient person, Tula admitted silently. But she was trying to fight her natural inclination—which would be grabbing Simon and shaking him until he admitted he loved her—so she could have the time to show Simon exactly how good they were together.

"Maybe this will work out, Nathan," she told the baby as she zipped up his tiny sweatshirt for their walk to the bookstore. "Maybe we will become a *real* family."

The baby laughed at the idea and clapped his hands together as if applauding her.

"That's my boy." She kissed him, then picked up the baby she thought of as her son and settled him into his stroller. "Now, Nathan, what do you say we go see the nice lady at the bookstore and talk about the signing this weekend?"

For days Simon had been living in two different worlds.

In one, he experienced a kind of happiness that he had never known before. In the other, there was a black cloud of misery hanging over his head, making him feel as though he was about to make the biggest mistake of his life.

He walked down the crowded sidewalk in the heart of downtown San Francisco and hardly noticed the bustle around him. His gaze fixed dead ahead, the expression on his face was ferocious enough to convince other pedestrians to give him a wide berth.

His mind raced with too many thoughts to process at once. Something he wasn't accustomed to at all. His concentration skills were nearly legendary. But even the inner workings of the Bradley department store chain couldn't keep him fixated for long anymore. That acknowledgment shook him to his bones. The Bradley chain had always been his focus. The one mainstay of his life. Rebuilding what the family had lost. Growing the company until it was the biggest of its kind in the country.

Those were tangible goals.

His entire life for the last ten years had been dedicated to making those dreams a reality. But lately, they weren't his only goals.

Tula.

Everything came back to her, he thought and waited impatiently for the light to change and the Walk symbol to flash green. Around him, a teenager danced along to whatever music he had plugged into his ears. A young mother swayed, keeping the baby in her arms happy. Taxis honked, someone shouted and the world, in general, kept spinning.

For everyone but him.

Simon knew he didn't have to go through with this. Didn't have to walk into the exclusive restaurant precisely at twelve-thirty and "accidentally" meet the man he'd waited years to take down. He knew he still had a chance to turn away from his plan. From the decision he had made before Tula became so damned important to him.

Tula.

She was there again. Front and center in his thoughts. Her short, soft hair. Her quick grin. That dimple that continued to devastate him every time he saw it flash in her cheek. She was there with her stories about lonely children befriending rabbits. She was there, rocking Nathan in the middle of the night. She was in the kitchen, dancing to the radio as she cooked. He saw her in her tiny house in Crystal Bay. So small, yet so full of life. Of love.

Tula had waltzed into his life and turned everything he had ever known upside down.

The light changed and he walked with the crowd, a part of them, yet separate.

For days now, he and Tula and Nathan had been what he had never thought to have…a family. Laughing with the baby in the evening, holding Tula all through the night and then waking up with her curled up against him every morning. It was enough to drive a man out of his mind.

This wasn't how Simon had planned for his life to go.

Never before had he made room in his thoughts for babies and bunnies and smart-mouthed women who kissed him as if he contained the last breath on earth. Now he couldn't imagine his life without any of them.

And he didn't damn well know what to do about it.

The wind off the ocean was icy, chilling the blood in his veins until he felt as cold and grim as his thoughts. Outside the restaurant, Simon actually paused and considered the situation.

If Mick was right, then going inside to face down Jacob would ruin whatever he might have with Tula. On the other hand, if he *didn't* go inside and nothing came of whatever was happening between him and Tula, then he had wasted his one opportunity to get back at a man he'd spent too many years hating.

Scrubbing one hand across the back of his neck,

Simon stood in the sea of constantly moving pedestrians like a boulder in the middle of a rushing stream. For the first time in his life, he wasn't sure what his next move should be.

For the first time ever, he wondered if he shouldn't be putting someone else ahead of his own needs.

"Make up your damn mind," he muttered, shifting his gaze to take in the wide windows and the diners seated in leather booths affording a view of downtown.

That's when he saw Jacob Hawthorne.

Everything in Simon went still as ice. The old man was lording it over a group of businessmen at his table. Seated like a king before supplicants, the old thief was clearly holding court. And who knew what he was up to? Who knew which company Jacob was trying to destroy now?

Thoughts of Tula rose up in Simon's mind as if his subconscious was combating what he was seeing. Reminding him of what he could have. What he might lose.

Tula. The daughter of his enemy. Simon shouldn't have been able to trust her. But he did. He shouldn't have cared about her. But he did.

Still, it wasn't enough, he told himself, already reaching for the door handle and tugging it open.

He owed it to his father. Hell, he owed it to *himself* to give Jacob the set down the man had practically been begging to receive for years.

And nothing was going to stop him.

Twelve

There were posters of her latest book cover standing on easels at the front entrance of the bookstore. Management had even put her picture on the sign announcing the author reading and signing that weekend. Cringing a little, Tula tried not to look at her own image.

"Ms. Barrons!"

She turned to smile as Barbara, the employee responsible for all of this, hurried over. "Hi, nice to see you again."

Barbara shook the hand Tula offered and then waved at the sign. "Do you approve?"

"It's very nice," she said, idly noting that she really needed a new publicity picture taken. "Thank you."

"Oh, it's no bother, believe me," Barbara told her. "We've sold so many of your books already, you'll be signing for hours this weekend."

"Now that *is* good news," Tula replied, reaching down to lift Nathan from his stroller when he started to complain. "It's okay, sweetie, we won't be long, then we'll go to the park," she promised.

"You have a beautiful son," Barbara cooed, reaching in to take one of Nathan's tiny hands in hers.

Pleased, Tula didn't correct her. Instead, she felt her own heart swell with longing, pride and love. She looked at the tiny boy in her arms and smiled when he gave her a toothless grin. Kissing him tenderly, she looked at Barbara and said simply, "Thank you."

Simon walked to Jacob's table, dismissing the hostess who tried to intercept him. His gaze locked on the old man; he paid no attention to the other diners or even to the three older men at Jacob's table.

All he could see was the man he'd waited years to get even with. The man who had destroyed Simon's father and nearly cost him the business his family had built over generations.

He stopped beside the table and looked down at the man who was his enemy. Tula had gotten her blue eyes from her father, but the difference was there was no warmth in Jacob's eyes. No silent sense of humor winking out at him. She was nothing like her father at all, Simon thought, wondering how someone as warm as Tula could have sprung from a man with ice in his veins.

"Bradley," the older man said, glancing at him with a sniff of distaste. "What are you doing here?"

"Thought we could have a chat, Jacob," Simon said, not bothering to acknowledge the other men at the table.

"I'm busy. Another time." Jacob turned to the man on his right.

"Actually, now works best for me," Simon said, keeping his voice low enough that only those at the table were privy to what he had to say.

The older man sighed dramatically, turned to face him and said, "Fine. What is it?"

For the first time, Simon glanced at the other men. "Maybe we should do this in private."

"I don't see any need for that," Jacob argued. "This is a scheduled business meeting. You're the intruder here."

Right again. It was only thanks to Mick's reluctantly given information that Simon had known where to find the old goat. Now he didn't argue, he merely turned his flat, no-negotiation stare on the other men at the table. It didn't take them long to excuse themselves and stand up.

"Five minutes," Jacob told them.

"I don't need even that long," Simon assured him as the three men left, heading for the bar.

The steak house was old, moneyed and exclusive. The walls were paneled in dark oak, the carpet was bloodred and the booths and chairs were overstuffed black leather. Candles flickered on every table and wall sconces burned with low-wattage bulbs, making the place seem like a well-decorated cave.

Simon took a seat opposite the old man and met that hard stare with one of his own. This was the moment he had waited for and he wanted to savor it. Jacob had taken something from him. Had tried to destroy Simon's father and almost had. Now Simon had taken something from Jacob.

Payback, the old man was about to learn, really was a bitch.

"What's this about?" Hawthorne leaned back in the seat and draped one arm negligently along the back of the booth. "Come to complain about my getting the property you wanted again? Because if that's it, I'm not interested. Ancient history."

"I'm not here to talk about your dubious business practices, Jacob," Simon told him.

"What you call dubious, I call smart. Efficient." The old man snorted. "Then if that's not what's chewing on you, what is it, boy? I'm a busy man. No time to waste."

"Fine. I'll get right to it then," Simon said, even while that voice in the back of his mind urged him to shut up, stand up and leave before it was too late. But looking into Jacob's eyes, seeing the barely concealed sneer of superiority on his face, made it impossible for Simon to listen.

"Well?" Impatience stained Jacob's tone.

"Just wanted you to know that while you were out stealing that property from me, I stole something from you."

"And what's that?"

"Your daughter." Simon hated himself for doing it, but he watched and waited for the old man's reaction. When it came, it wasn't what he had expected.

Those icy blue eyes frosted over and emptied in the space of a single heartbeat. "I have no daughter."

"You do," Simon argued, leaning forward, lowering his voice. "Tula. She's at my house right now."

Jacob speared him with a hard look. "Tallulah Barrons is not my daughter. Not anymore. If that's what you came for, we're finished."

"You'd deny your own flesh and blood?" Shocked in spite of how badly he had always thought of Jacob Hawthorne, Simon could only stare at him.

Jacob looked away and signaled for the hostess. When she arrived, he said, "Please tell my guests I'm ready to continue our meeting. You'll find them in the bar."

"Yes, sir," she said and hurried off.

"You really don't give a damn about Tula, do you?" Simon hadn't moved. Couldn't force himself to look away from the old man's eyes.

"Why the hell should I?" Jacob countered. "She made her choice. Now what she does—or," he added snidely, "*who* she does it with—is nothing to me. We're done here, Bradley."

Stunned to his bones, Simon realized he actually felt dirty.

Just sitting at the same table with the man. Strange, but he had always pictured the moment of his revenge as tasting sweet. Being satisfying in a soul-deep way. He'd imagined that he would be vindicated. That he would walk away from Hawthorne, head held high, secure in the knowledge that he had bested the old thief. That he had *won*.

Finally.

Instead, years of anticipation fell flat. He felt as though he'd climbed down into the gutter to wrestle a rat for a bone. Mick had been right, of course. Simon had lowered himself to Jacob Hawthorne's level and now he was left with a bitter taste in his mouth and what felt like an oil spill on his soul.

Thoughts of Tula ran through his mind like a soft,

cool breeze on a miserable day. She was the openhearted person he had never been. She was all of the smiles and warmth and joy that he had never known. Everything about her was the opposite of everything he was. Everything her parents had been. Somehow, she was the very heart that he hadn't even realized was missing from his life.

And he'd betrayed her.

He had used her for leverage against a man who didn't even see what an amazing woman his daughter was. But if Jacob Hawthorne was blind, then so had Simon been. Now, though, he could see. Now that it was too late.

Standing up slowly, Simon looked down at the man. Shaking his head, he had the last word as he told Jacob, "You know, I've wasted a lot of years hating your guts. Turns out, you just weren't worth it."

Simon found Tula in the living room, curled up on the window seat reading. She looked up when he walked into the room and the smile she gave him, complete with dimple, tore at his insides. He had made up his mind to tell her the truth. All of it. But he knew the moment he did, everything would be ruined. Over. And he would have to live with the knowledge that he had hurt the one person in the world he shouldn't have.

"Simon? What's wrong?" She came up off the window seat and walked to him, concern in her eyes.

He held up one hand to hold her off, not trusting himself to go through with this confession if she came into his arms. Once he had the feel of her against him again, he might not be able to force himself to let her go. And that's what he had to do.

"I saw your father today," he blurted, knowing there was no easy way to say any of this.

Her jaw dropped and her blue eyes suddenly looked wary. "I didn't realize you knew him."

"Oh, yeah," Simon said tightly. "Remember when I told you about the man who nearly stole this house from my father? The man who stole a piece of property out from under my nose?"

"My father."

"Yeah." Simon walked past her and headed to the wet bar. There he poured himself a short scotch and tossed it down his throat like a gulp of medicine designed to take the inner chill away.

"See, when I found out who you were," he mused aloud, staring down at the crystal glass in his hand before shifting his gaze to hers, "I had the bright idea of somehow using you to get back at your father."

She actually winced. He saw the tiny reaction and, even from across the room, he felt her pain and hated himself for causing it. But he couldn't stop now. Had to tell her everything. Didn't someone say that confession was good for the soul? He didn't think so. It was more like ripping your soul out, piece by piece.

"I told him today that we were together." He waited for a reaction. The only sign she had heard him was the expression of resigned sorrow on her face.

"I could have told you," she finally said into the strained silence, "that he wouldn't care. My father disowned me when I chose to, as he put it, 'waste my brain writing books for sniveling brats.'"

"Tula…" He heard the old pain in her voice and saw her misery shining in her eyes. Everything in him pushed at him to go to her. To hold her. To…love her as she deserved to be loved. But he knew she wouldn't welcome his touch any longer and that brought a whole new world of pain crashing through him.

"He's an idiot," Simon muttered, then added, "and so was I. I didn't want to tell you any of this, but you had the right to know."

"Oh," she said sadly, "*now* I had the right to know."

He gritted his teeth and still managed to say, "I didn't mean to hurt you."

"No," she agreed, "probably not. It was just a by-product of you going after what you wanted. In a way, I'm not surprised. I knew when I first met you that you were like him. Like my father. Both of you only know about business and using people."

He took a step toward her, but stopped when she moved back, instinctively. How could he argue with that simple truth? Maybe, he told himself, he was even worse than her father. He had actually *seen* Tula for who she really was and had lied to her, used her, anyway.

Simon thought back to his meeting with Jacob Hawthorne. He had seen firsthand just what kind of man the old pirate was. And unless he made some changes in his own life, Simon knew he would end up just as cold and ruthless and empty as Jacob was.

Choosing his words carefully, he said, "I know you have no reason to believe me, but I'm not the man I was when you first came here. More, I don't want to be that man."

"Simon," she said softly, shaking her head.

"Let me finish." He took a breath, and said, "There are a lot of things I should say to you, but maybe I don't have the right anymore. So instead, I think the only way to prove to you that I'm not who you think I am, is to let you go."

"What?"

"Hell," he laughed shortly, shoving one hand through his hair with enough strength to yank it all out. "It's the only decent thing to do." He looked into her eyes. "We both know I'm ready to take care of Nathan. I'll hire the best nanny in the country to help me out. And you can go home. Get away from here. From me. It's the right thing to do."

Tula felt the world tip out from under her feet. She swayed under the blow of the unexpected slap. Bad enough to hear that the man she loved had only been pretending to care so that he could use her against the father that didn't give a damn about her anyway. Bad enough to know that her hopes and dreams had just been shattered at her feet.

Now, she was being sent away. From the baby. From Simon.

For her own good.

Pain was a living, breathing entity, and it roared from inside her as it settled in, making a permanent home in the black emptiness where her heart used to be. Hurt, humiliated and just plain tired of being used by the very people in her life she should have been able to count on, Tula sighed.

"Don't you see, Simon?" she whispered sadly. "Even in this, you're still acting like my father."

"No," he argued, but she cut him off because she just didn't want to hear anything else he had to say.

"Letting me go isn't about *me*. It's about *you*. About how you feel about what you did. About assuaging some sense of honor you believe you've lost."

"Tula, that's not—"

"What if I didn't want to go?" she asked, watching him. "What then?"

Naturally, he didn't have an answer for her. But then, it didn't matter, because Tula wasn't waiting for one. It was too late for them and she knew it. She had to go, whether leaving would rip her heart to pieces or not.

Softly, she said, "Nathan's asleep upstairs. If it's all the same to you, I'll leave now, before he wakes up. I don't think I can say goodbye to him."

"Tula, damn it, at least let me—"

"You've done enough, Simon," she told him, turning for the stairs. "Have your lawyer contact me. I'll sign whatever papers are necessary to turn over custody of Nathan to you. And Simon," she added, "promise me you'll love him enough for both of us."

Over the next few days, Simon and Nathan were miserable together.

Nothing was the same. Simon couldn't work—he didn't give a damn about mergers or acquisitions or the price of the company stock. He hated having Mick telling him *I told you so* every five minutes. The memory of Tula in his house was so strong that her absence made the whole place seem cavernous and as empty as a black hole.

He and his son were lost without the only woman either of them wanted.

Nathan cried continuously for the only mother he remembered. Simon comforted him, but it was a hollow effort since he knew exactly how the baby felt. And there was no comfort for either of them as long as Tula wasn't there.

Simon hadn't even hired a nanny. He didn't want some other woman holding Nathan. He wanted Tula back home. With them. Where she belonged. Every day without her was emptier than the one before. His dreams were filled with images of her and his arms ached to hold her.

He had fallen in love with the one woman who probably couldn't stand the sight of him. He had had a family, damn it, and he wanted it back. Yes, he had been a first-class idiot. A prize moron. But Tula had a heart big enough, he hoped, to forgive even him.

If she hadn't promised to do this signing, Tula didn't know if she would have had the nerve to return to the city. Used to be she avoided San Francisco because there were memories of her father here. Now it was so much more.

Nathan and Simon were only blocks from this bookstore. They were in that Victorian that she'd come to love and think of as her own. They were no doubt settling into life with a nanny and she wondered if either of them missed her as desperately as she missed them.

She sat cross-legged in the middle of the "reading rug" at the bookstore and looked at the shining, expectant faces surrounding her. Parents stood on the periphery, watching their children, enjoying their excitement. And Tula knew that she couldn't simply walk away from Simon and Nathan.

Yes, Simon had hurt her. Desperately. But he had told her everything, hadn't he? It couldn't have been easy for him to admit to what he had done. It said something that he'd eventually been honest with her.

Through her pain, through her misery, one truth

had rung clear over the last few days. Despite what had happened, she still loved Simon. And when the book signing was over, she was going to see him. She would just show up at the house and tell Simon Bradley that she loved him. Maybe he wouldn't care. And maybe, if she took a chance, they could start fresh and rebuild their family.

With that thought in mind, she smiled at the kids and asked, "Are you ready to hear about the Lonely Bunny and how he found a friend?"

"Yes!" A dozen childish voices shouting in unison made her laugh and she felt lighter in her soul than she had since walking out of Simon's life.

Opening the book, Tula began to read and for the next half hour gave her young audience her complete attention. When the story of the Lonely Bunny and a white kitten ended, children applauded and parents picked up copies of her books.

Tula smiled to herself as she signed her books and spent a minute or two with each of the children, giving them Lonely Bunny stickers to fix to their shirts. She was enjoying herself even while a corner of her mind worried over going to see Simon.

Through the noise and confusion, Tula felt someone watching her. Her skin prickled and her heartbeat quickened in reaction even before she looked up—directly into Simon's dark brown eyes. Instead of one of his sharply cut business suits, he was wearing jeans and a T-shirt with the Lonely Bunny logo. He held Nathan in his arms and she noticed that the baby wore a matching T-shirt.

Tula laughed and held her breath, afraid to read too much into this surprising visit. Maybe he had simply come to give her the chance to say goodbye to Nathan. Maybe the emotions she read in Simon's eyes were only regret and fondness. And maybe she would make herself nuts if she didn't find out.

She stood up slowly, never taking her gaze from his. Her heart doing somersaults in her chest, Tula tried to speak, but her mouth was dry. When Nathan reached out pudgy arms to her, she took him, grateful to feel his warm, solid weight as he snuggled in with a happy sigh.

Simon shrugged and said, "I, uh, saw the sign out front advertising that you would be here today."

"And you came," she whispered, running one hand up and down the baby's back.

"Of course I came," Simon said, gaze locked with hers, silently telling her everything she had ever wanted to hear. It was all there for her to read. He wasn't hiding anything anymore. So neither would she.

"I was going to come and see you after the signing."

He smiled and moved closer. "You were?"

"I had something to tell you," she said.

He must have seen what he needed to see written on her face because he spoke quickly. "Let me go first. I have so much I want to say to you, Tula."

She laughed a little and glanced around at the kids and their parents, all of them watching with interest. "Now?"

He looked at their audience, then shrugged them off as inconsequential. "Right here, right now."

To her amazement, he went down on one knee in front of her and looked up into her eyes. "Simon…"

"Me first," he said with a smile and shake of his head.

"Tula, I can't live without you. I tried and I just can't do it. You're the air I breathe. You're the heart of me. You're everything I need and can't do without."

Someone in the audience sighed but neither of them paid any attention.

"Oh, Simon—" Tears filled her eyes. She blinked them away because she didn't want to miss a moment of this.

He took her hand and slowly stood up to face her. "I love you. I should have told you that first. But I'll make up for that by saying it often. I love you. I love you."

Tula laughed a little, then harder when Nathan gurgled and laughed along with her. "I love you, too," she told Simon, her heart feeling as though it could pop out of her chest and fly around the room. "That's what I was coming to tell you. I love you, Simon."

"Marry me," he said quickly as if half-afraid she would change her mind. "Marry me. Be my wife and Nathan's mother. Be with me so neither of us ever has to be like your Lonely Bunny again."

"Yes, Simon," Tula said, moving into the circle of his arms. "Oh, yes."

As he stood in the bookstore, with his entire world held close to him, Simon listened to the cheers from the watching crowd. Staring down into Tula's blue eyes, he bent to kiss her and knew that like the Velveteen Rabbit she had told him about, it hurt to become real.

But it was worth it.

Epilogue

A year and a half later, Simon urged, "Push, Tula! Don't stop now, you're almost there!"

"You push for awhile, okay?" she asked, letting her head drop to the pillow. "I'm taking a break."

"Hey," the doctor called out from the foot of the bed, "nobody gets a coffee break yet!"

Simon laughed, planted a hard, fast kiss on Tula's forehead and said, "As soon as this is over, we're *both* taking a break. And, I swear, we'll never do this again."

"Oh, yes, we will," she told him with a sudden gasp. "I want at least six kids."

"You're killin' me," Simon said with a groan. He added, "Come on, honey, one more push."

Tula grinned up at him despite the pain he could see shining in her eyes. "Nag, nag, nag..." Then her features stiffened and she took a breath. "Here it comes again."

Simon had never been so terrified and so excited at once in his life. His gorgeous wife was the bravest, strongest, most miraculous human being in the world. He was humbled by her and so damn grateful to have her in his life.

"You're a warrior, Tula. You can do this. I'm right here, honey, just get it done." And *please* do it fast, he added in a silent prayer.

Mick had warned him that labor was hard on a husband. But Simon had had no idea what it would be like to stand beside the woman he loved and watch her suffer. But typically Tula, she had insisted on going through with this naturally.

Silently, Simon promised that if they ever did this again, God help him, he was going to demand that she take drugs. Or he would.

"Here we go," Doctor Liz Haney called out in encouragement. "Just a little more, Tula!"

She bore down, gritted her teeth and took Simon's hand in a crushing grip that he swore later had pulverized his bones. But then a thin, wailing cry split the air. Tula laughed, delighted, and Simon took his first relieved breath in what felt like months.

"It's a boy!" Doctor Liz reached out and laid the red-faced, squalling, beautiful child across Tula's chest.

"He's amazing," Simon said, "just like his mother."

"Hello, little Gavin," Tula said with a tired sigh as she stroked her newborn son's back. "We've been waiting for you. Your big brother is going to be so excited to meet you."

Simon's heart was so full it was a wonder he could

draw a breath. His world was perfect. Tula was safe and they had another beautiful son.

His exhausted wife looked up at him. "You should call Mick and Katie to check on Nathan—and to tell them our little Gavin is here."

"I will," Simon said, bending down to kiss her reverently. "Have I mentioned lately that I love you?"

"Only every day," she whispered back, her eyes tired but bright with happiness and satisfaction at a job well done.

"We'll just take the baby and clean him up," one of the nurses said, scooping Gavin into her arms.

Tula watched them go, then smiled at Simon when his cell phone chirped, alerting him to an incoming email. "I thought you were turning that off," she said.

"I meant to but I got distracted," he said, grinning as he read the email. "Hey, this isn't about me," he told her. "Your agent emailed to say your latest book just hit the *New York Times* list! Congratulations, honey."

Tula grinned. As exciting as that news was, it couldn't compare to what she felt every day of her life. Taking Simon's hand, she said, "I knew this book would do well. How could it miss with that title?"

He grinned and leaned over her for another kiss. *"Lonely Bunny Finds a Family,"* he whispered, then added, "I hope he's as happy as I am with mine."

* * * * *

COMING NEXT MONTH

Available February 8, 2011

#2065 THE BILLIONAIRE GETS HIS WAY
Elizabeth Bevarly

#2066 SEDUCED: THE UNEXPECTED VIRGIN
Emily McKay
The Takeover

#2067 THE BOSS'S BABY AFFAIR
Tessa Radley
Billionaires and Babies

#2068 TAMING THE VIP PLAYBOY
Katherine Garbera
Miami Nights

#2069 TO TEMPT A SHEIKH
Olivia Gates
Pride of Zohayd

#2070 MILLION-DOLLAR AMNESIA SCANDAL
Rachel Bailey

SDCNM0111

Spotlight on

Classic

Quintessential, modern love stories that are romance at its finest.

See the next page to enjoy a sneak peek from the Harlequin® Romance series.

CATCLASSHR10

Harlequin Romance author Donna Alward is loved for her gorgeous rancher heroes.

Meet Wyatt as he's confronted by both a precious little pink bundle left on his doorstep and his neighbor Elli who's going to show him the ropes....

Introducing
PROUD RANCHER, PRECIOUS BUNDLE

THE SQUAWKING QUIETED as Elli picked the baby up, and Wyatt turned around, trying hard to ignore the feelings of inadequacy as Darcy immediately stopped fussing.

"Maybe she's uncomfortable. What do you think, sweetheart?" Elli turned her conversation to the baby.

"What do you think is wrong?" Wyatt asked, putting the coffee pot back on the burner.

A strange look passed over Elli's face, one that looked like guilt and panic. But it was gone quickly. "I couldn't say," she replied.

"But you were so good with her this afternoon." Wyatt put his hands on his hips.

"Lucky, that's all. I just...remembered a few things." The same strange look flitted over her features once more.

Wyatt took the coffee to the table. "You fooled me. You looked like you knew exactly what you were doing." So much so that Wyatt had felt completely inept. A feeling he despised. He was used to being the one in control.

Elli and Darcy walked the length of the kitchen and back. After a few moments, she admitted, "I haven't really cared for a baby before. The things I thought of were simply things I'd heard about. Not from experience, Mr. Black."

Her chin jutted up, closing the subject but making him

HREXP0211

want to ask the questions now pulsing through his mind. But then he remembered the old saying—*Don't look a gift horse in the mouth.* He'd benefit from whatever insight she had and be glad of it.

"I don't really know what babies need," he said. "I fed her, patted her back like you did, walked her to sleep, but every time I put her down…"

Wyatt almost groaned. Of course. He'd forgotten one important thing. He'd been so focused on getting the formula the right temperature that he'd forgotten to check her diaper. Not that he had any clue what to do there either.

Pulling calves and shoveling out stalls was far less intimidating than one tiny newborn.

"She's probably due for a diaper change, isn't she." He tried to sound nonchalant. This was a perfect opportunity. Elli must know how to change a diaper. He could simply watch her so he'd know better for the next time.

Instead, Elli came around the corner of the counter and placed Darcy back in his arms. "Here you go, Uncle Wyatt," she said lightly. "You get diaper duty. I'll fix the coffee. Cream and sugar?"

Oh boy, Wyatt thought, looking down into Darcy's pursed face, his smug plan blown to smithereens. He was in for it now.